Christy® Juvenile Fiction Series

VOLUME FOUR

Christy® Juvenile Fiction Series

Christy® Juvenile Fiction Series
VOLUME FOUR

Stage Fright
Goodbye, Sweet Prince
Brotherly Love

Catherine Marshall
adapted by C. Archer

Tommy nelson
A Division of Thomas Nelson Publishers
Since 1798
www.thomasnelson.com

VOLUME FOUR
Stage Fright
Goodbye, Sweet Prince
Brotherly Love
in the *Christy*® Juvenile Fiction Series

Copyright © 1997
by the Estate of Catherine Marshall LeSourd

The *Christy*® Juvenile Fiction Series is based on
Christy® by Catherine Marshall LeSourd © 1967
by Catherine Marshall LeSourd © renewed
1997 by Marshall-LeSourd, L.L.C.

The *Christy*® name and logo are officially registered
trademarks of Marshall-LeSourd, L.L.C.

All characters, themes, plots, and subplots portrayed in this
book are the licensed property of Marshall-LeSourd, L.L.C.

Published in Nashville, Tennessee, by Tommy Nelson®,
a Division of Thomas Nelson, Inc.

ISBN 1-4003-0775-9

Printed in the United States of America

05 06 07 08 09 BANTA 9 8 7 6 5 4 3 2 1

Stage Fright

The Characters

CHRISTY RUDD HUDDLESTON, a nineteen-year-old schoolteacher in Cutter Gap.

CHRISTY'S STUDENTS:
    CREED ALLEN, age nine.
    LITTLE BURL ALLEN, age six.
    BESSIE COBURN, age twelve.
    LIZETTE HOLCOMBE, age fifteen.
    MOUNTIE O'TEALE, age ten.
    RUBY MAE MORRISON, age thirteen.
    MABEL, age eight.

DAVID GRANTLAND, the young minister.

IDA GRANTLAND, David's sister and the mission housekeeper.

ALICE HENDERSON, a Quaker missionary who helped start the mission at Cutter Gap.

DR. NEIL MACNEILL, the physician of the Cove.

MRS. CORA GRAY, the doctor's aunt from Knoxville.

ROBERT GRAY, deceased husband of Cora.

JOSEPH MCPRATT, JR., the boy who starred with Christy in a high school production of *Romeo and Juliet*.

JEB SPENCER, Cutter Gap's finest dulcimer player.

PETER MULBERRY, friend of Dr. MacNeill during medical school.

JAMES BRILEY, former medical school classmate of Dr. MacNeill.

MEMBERS OF THE KNOXVILLE PLAYERS:
ARABELLA DEVAINE, costume and set designer.
OLIVER FLUMP, assistant director.
GILROY GANNON, actor.
MARYLOU MARSH, Arabella's assistant.
VERNON MARSH, Marylou's brother.
SARAH MCGEORGE, actress.
PANSY TROTMAN, understudy.

MABEL, one of the schoolhouse's resident hogs.

❧ One ❧

"Has anyone seen Goldilocks?" Christy Huddleston called as she surveyed her crowded schoolroom.

With seventy students in one room, things were always a little disorganized. Today, however, the room was in chaos.

Of course, it was a very special day. Today was the dress rehearsal of the school's first play, *Goldilocks and the Three Bears.*

Christy climbed onto her desk and clapped her hands. "Attention, everyone!" A few students paused. Christy tried again. "Children!" she called, trying to make herself heard over the babble of excited voices. "What did I tell you about the director of a play?"

"The director gets to boss everybody else around," answered Creed Allen. Creed, who was nine, had been cast in the role of the father bear, or, as the children called him, "Pa Bear."

He paused to adjust the beaver pelt that comprised his costume. Christy had helped Creed tie it around his head with a piece of string. He didn't look anything like a bear, of course, but that didn't matter. As Christy had been teaching them all month, the theater was about make-believe.

Teaching at the mission school here in Cutter Gap always meant working without the usual supplies. But by now, Christy had grown skilled at making do with very little. In fact, she'd chosen the story of the three bears because it required so few props. Christy had written the simple play herself.

Gazing around the room, she felt certain that the schoolhouse was going to work nicely as a theater. (It already served as the church on Sundays.) Christy had talked Miss Ida, who ran the mission house, into parting with a worn sheet.

David Grantland, the young minister for the Cutter Gap mission and Miss Ida's brother, had strung a rope across part of the room. With a little ingenuity, Christy had a curtain for her makeshift stage.

"All right. I see my three bears," Christy called loudly.

"Six bears, Teacher," said Ruby Mae Morrison. Thirteen-year-old Ruby Mae had been wearing her bear costume for days now. The costume was really nothing more than a huge brown coat, far too large for Ruby Mae. She'd found the coat in a box of clothes donated to the mission by a church in Christy's hometown. Christy was allowing Ruby Mae to use it for the play, as long as she promised to return it to the box in good shape.

"Ain't but just three bears in the play," said Bessie Coburn, one of Ruby Mae's best friends. "You all is just underbears."

"Understudies, Bessie," Christy corrected.

"We's proper bears!" Ruby Mae exclaimed. She growled menacingly and clawed at the air, just the way Christy had instructed during "bear lessons" yesterday. "We's the ones who'll take your place if'n somebody eats you up, Ma Bear!"

Bessie sighed as she adjusted her bear costume. "I still don't see why we have to do such a babyish play."

"I wanted to do a play with a plot that even the youngest children could understand, Bessie," Christy explained. "If this first play goes well, maybe we can try something more complicated next time." She smiled. "Who knows? We could even stage a play by Shakespeare."

"Shakespeare?" Bessie repeated.

"He was a very fine writer who lived a long time ago," Christy replied. "In the meantime, I want you to be the very best bear you can possibly be, all right?"

While Bessie and Ruby Mae engaged in a mock bear fight, Christy once again clapped her hands. "Let's everyone take our places for the final scene," she called.

Finally, everyone paid attention. Christy watched in delight as the children rushed to their places. In all her months of teaching, she'd never seen them so excited about a project.

When she'd told Miss Alice Henderson, the Quaker missionary who'd helped start the mission school, about her plan to stage a play, Miss Alice had shaken her head. "Are you sure you're not biting off more than you can chew, Christy?" she'd asked. "After all, you've only been teaching a short time. Maybe you should save such a big production for next year."

"But I loved the theater when I was going to school," Christy had replied. "I know the children will love it, too."

And they had. She'd somehow found a way to give each child an important part to play, even if it wasn't on stage. They'd built simple sets. They'd learned about how to behave in the audience. And they'd even learned a little bit about acting.

"Places, everyone!" Christy called. "Is Goldilocks in position?"

"Yes'm, Miz Christy," Creed said, grinning. He pointed to the smallest bed, where a figure lay covered by a threadbare sheet.

Christy had decided that Lizette Holcombe should play Goldilocks, but it had been a controversial casting choice. Because Lizette had brown hair, many of the other students had objected. But Lizette had a real presence on stage. Besides, she was one of the few students in class who could memorize all the lines.

"Little Burl, the curtain!" Christy called.

Little Burl Allen pulled back the sheet that separated the desks and benches from the stage area.

"Pa Bear," Christy whispered loudly. "Your line!"

Creed cleared his throat. He lumbered toward the first bed. The bed was made of a few crude boards that the older students had nailed together with David's help.

Creed yanked on the worn sheet covering the bed. "I declare!" he cried. "Somebody's been a-sleepin' in this here bed!"

Bessie went over to the second bed, crawling on her hands and knees. "And if I don't miss my guess, somebody's been a-snorin' away in my bed, too!"

A long pause followed. Mountie O'Teale, a shy ten-year-old, inched her way toward the center of the stage. Her face had been darkened with a piece of coal—Christy's version of stage makeup.

Mountie suffered from a speech impediment, but with Christy's help, she'd made a lot of progress. Christy had hoped that giving Mountie a speaking role would boost the little girl's confidence. Now, seeing her nervous expression, she wasn't so sure.

"Go ahead, Mountie," Christy said gently.

Mountie started to speak. She glanced back at Creed, who gave a nod.

"Some . . . somebody's been . . ." Mountie began.

"Keep going, Mountie," Christy whispered. "You can do it!"

"Some . . . somebody's been a-sleepin' in my bed," Mountie said, "and—and—"

Several students snickered. "Hush," Christy said sternly. "Go on, Mountie. Pull on the sheet and say your line."

Mountie went to the smallest bed and grasped the edge of the sheet. Goldilocks lay hidden, breathing steadily.

"Somebody's been a-sleepin' in my bed," Mountie repeated, "and here she is!"

She yanked on the sheet. For a moment, all was still. Then, suddenly, uproarious laughter filled the room.

Lizette was not on the bed.

In her place was Mabel, one of the resident hogs who lived under the schoolhouse. She snored away, undisturbed by the commotion around her. Lizette emerged from the spot behind the bed where she'd been hiding. "Looks to me like ol' Goldilocks has been eatin' *way* too much of our porridge!" she exclaimed.

Mabel opened one eye. She looked over at Lizette and gave a disgusted snort.

Mountie ran over to Christy, her face alight. "Did we fool you, Teacher?"

"I'll say!" Christy said, shaking her head. "It was a wonderful joke, children."

"When you was in school plays," Ruby Mae asked, "did you have this much fun, Miz Christy?"

Christy smiled. "Those were some of the best days of my life, Ruby Mae. But to tell you the truth, you are the finest cast I've ever had the pleasure to work with." She gave Mountie a hug. "Now, how about if we rehearse the whole play from the beginning? Only this time, let's try it without Mabel in the starring role!"

❧ TWO ❧

That afternoon when the children had left, Christy stood on the empty "stage." They'd truly seemed to enjoy themselves today, and so had she. On days like this, she loved teaching with all her heart. She just knew she was doing the work God had always intended for her to do.

Of course, she hadn't always been so sure she wanted to be a teacher. In fact, in high school back in Asheville, North Carolina, Christy had been certain that she was destined for the New York stage. Well, maybe not *certain*. But she had dreamed about it from time to time, especially after her performance in *Romeo and Juliet*. Everyone said she'd been the best Juliet in the history of Asheville High School.

She could still see the lovely balcony set.

She could still remember her silken gown, the one her mother had lovingly stitched for her. She could still remember every line as if it were yesterday. . . .

"O Romeo, Romeo, wherefore art thou Romeo?" Christy whispered.

Slowly she recited the words she knew so well, her voice swelling with feeling. She clasped her hands before her, eyes closed, as she repeated Shakespeare's famous lines as if they were her own.

Suddenly a familiar voice met her ears. "But, soft, what light through yonder window breaks? It is the east, and Juliet is the sun."

Christy's eyes flew open. Doctor MacNeill was standing in the doorway, arms crossed over his chest. He was a big, handsomely rugged man. His curly hair was unruly, and his hazel eyes were accented by smile lines. He stood there with an amused expression on his face.

"Neil!" Christy cried, her face burning with embarrassment. "How . . . how long have you been standing there?"

The doctor made his way past the maze of desks. "Long enough to tell you've been hiding your true talent from the rest of us. That was quite moving, if I do say so myself. Although I'm no theater critic."

"No Shakespeare buff, either," Christy replied. "You got your line wrong."

13

"I was overwhelmed by your delivery," the doctor said. His voice was teasing, but she could see the affection in his eyes. Doctor MacNeill had made no secret about his feelings for Christy. Still, he often hid them behind a wall of teasing and humor.

"I take it you're saying I'm no great Romeo?" the doctor inquired as he helped Christy move some of the props.

"Well, let's just say you're an improvement over the Romeo I starred with in high school— Joseph McPratt, Jr. He tended to spit when he delivered his lines. Especially the romantic ones."

The doctor clucked his tongue. "How unfortunate."

"Oh, well. I guess my career as an actress was doomed before it even took off."

"How's the play shaping up?"

Christy draped a sheet over one of the beds. "We had a last-minute cast change today. Mabel stood in for Lizette in the role of Goldilocks. It was quite a performance."

"She can be a bit of a ham, if you know what I mean." The doctor grinned. "You know, all of Cutter Gap's looking forward to the show tomorrow afternoon. I hope my Aunt Cora makes it here in time. She'd get a real kick out of it."

"She's due to get in this evening, isn't she?"

"It depends on the roads. With all the rain we've had lately, it's pretty slow going. It'll be good to see her. It's been almost six years."

"Well, I'm not sure a woman from a town as sophisticated as Knoxville will be all that impressed with our version of the theater."

"Oh, Aunt Cora loves the theater in any form. Did I tell you she directs plays for the Knoxville Players?"

Christy gasped. "Neil! Your aunt directs the Knoxville Players and you forgot to *tell* me? They're the finest acting company in Tennessee!" She squeezed his arm. "And you forgot to *tell* me?"

"It slipped my mind," Doctor MacNeill shrugged. "And let go of my arm, woman. You're cutting off the circulation."

"This is terrible. She's going to see our pathetic little play and laugh and laugh," Christy moaned. "Neil, don't let her come. Promise me you won't let her come. If I know she's in the audience, I'll be petrified."

The doctor laughed. "Christy, you're not acting in the play. A bunch of children are— children who never even heard the word *play* till you introduced it to them. And I think my aunt can tell the difference between the Cutter Gap production of *Goldilocks and the Three Bears* and Shakespeare."

"You're right," Christy admitted. "I don't

15

know what got into me. Sorry. I suppose I always thought maybe I'd star in a real play someday. . . ." She gave an embarrassed smile. "It's crazy, I know."

"Not at all. You forget I just witnessed your brilliant performance as Juliet."

"You're just being sweet."

"No, I'm just being honest." The doctor dropped to one knee. "Let's see if I still remember my college English class . . ." He cleared his throat, grasped Christy's hands in his and began to recite more lines:

> *Good night, good night! Parting is such*
> *sweet sorrow,*
> *That I shall say good night till it be morrow.*

Just then, David appeared in the doorway. He took one look at the doctor on his knees and loudly cleared his throat. "Excuse me for interrupting." He looked at Doctor MacNeill. "I came to tell you your aunt's just arrived at the mission house." He paused, scratching his head. "What exactly *am* I interrupting, anyway?"

Quickly, Doctor MacNeill got to his feet. "Just some terribly bad acting, I'm afraid, Reverend. I was doing my best to impress Christy with my Shakespeare."

David rolled his eyes. "In my experience, it takes more than that to impress Christy."

"Actually, I wasn't very impressed," Christy said. She winked at David. "The sad truth is, Neil, you were reciting *Juliet's* lines."

ᲐᲛ Three ᲑᲛ

So, Neil tells me you're a bit of a theater buff yourself, Christy," the doctor's aunt said that evening at dinner.

"She's the best director in Cutter Gap," exclaimed Ruby Mae, who lived at the mission house with Christy and Miss Ida. "'Course, factually speakin', she's the *only* one."

Cora Gray laughed loudly. "Ruby Mae, my dear, that's the best kind of director to be. Too many cooks spoil the broth, if you get my meaning."

"Truth to tell, I don't rightly follow you—" Ruby Mae began.

"Remember the other day, Ruby Mae," Christy said, "when you tried to convince me we should change the name of our play to *Goldilocks and the Six Bears* so that the understudies could perform, too? That's what Aunt Cora means by 'too many cooks.'"

"I weren't cookin'. I was directin'," Ruby Mae muttered as she reached for the bowl of Miss Ida's mashed potatoes.

Doctor MacNeil's aunt was so down-to-earth and charming that Christy already felt like she'd known her forever. She was a plump, animated woman with vivid blue eyes and a full-throated laugh you could hear in the next county. From the minute she'd arrived, she'd insisted that everyone call her "Aunt Cora."

"Aunt Cora, you'll be interested to hear that Christy once starred in *Romeo and Juliet*," the doctor said.

"So did your nephew," David added wryly. "I caught a bit of his performance this afternoon."

Doctor MacNeill pretended to pout. "Personally, I thought I made a riveting Juliet."

"I was just in a high school play, Aunt Cora," Christy explained quickly. "It was nothing, really."

"Right now, the Knoxville Players is working on a production of *Romeo and Juliet*," said Aunt Cora. "There's nothing tougher than Shakespeare."

"I wish I could see it," Christy said. "It's been so long since I've watched a real play. Not since I was living in Asheville."

"Cutter Gap doesn't get much in the way of the arts," Miss Alice explained with a smile. "That's why we're all so excited about Christy's play."

"Theater is my great love," Aunt Cora said. "When those curtains part and the lights dim, it's simply magical."

Christy couldn't help sighing. "That's how it always felt to me, too," she said. "I actually used to dream . . ." She hesitated, suddenly self-conscious.

"Dream what, dear?" Aunt Cora asked gently.

Christy shrugged. "Oh, you know—silly things. I dreamed that I'd someday be in a real play on a real stage."

"That was my very dream when I was growing up!" Aunt Cora said with a smile. "Don't forget: 'We are such stuff as dreams are made on.'" She winked at Ruby Mae. "That's from another one of Shakespeare's plays."

"He sure did write a heap," Ruby Mae said.

"I suppose he was a bit of a dreamer himself." Aunt Cora took a sip of her tea. "I like to think we all are."

"Oh, I got powerful plenty o' dreams," said Ruby Mae. "I want to be a mama in a big house in a fancy city, like Asheville—maybe even Knoxville. And I'll have me a golden horse, faster 'n lightnin'."

Aunt Cora nodded. "Those are fine dreams, Ruby Mae," she said.

"How about the rest o' you?" Ruby Mae asked. "Miss Alice, I'll bet you got yourself all kinds o' fine dreams."

Miss Alice considered. "That's a good question. I have lots of dreams, I suppose. To begin with, I dream of bringing medicine and learning and hope to every last person in these mountains." She grinned. "And of course, there's my long-held aspiration to learn to play the dulcimer."

"Why, Miss Alice, I'm sure Jeb Spencer would learn you to play, if'n you just asked him," Ruby Mae exclaimed.

"It's true, Miss Alice," Christy added. "Jeb's taught all of his children how to play. And it's such a lovely instrument."

Christy could still remember the first time she'd heard Jeb play the dulcimer. It was a box-like instrument with four strings, a slender waist and heart-shaped holes. The sweet music it made sounded as if it had been sent straight from heaven.

"How about you, Preacher?" Ruby Mae asked. "What's your dream?"

David combed back his straight, dark hair with his fingers. He thought for a moment before answering. "Well, to tell you the truth, Ruby Mae," he said, "I wouldn't mind seeing more of the world someday. Paris. London.

The mysterious Far East." He shrugged. "Of course, it'll probably never happen. It's hard to imagine having the time, let alone the money. . . ."

"You can't go a-thinkin' that way, Preacher," Ruby Mae scolded. She reached across the table to snare the last of Miss Ida's flaky biscuits. "You gotta keep hopin'. That's the fun o' dreamin'."

"Ruby Mae's right," Miss Alice agreed. "When I told people I was going to help start a mission here in the Great Smokies, you should have heard their reactions. They said I was doomed to fail." She grinned. "Some even said I was crazy. But you have to dream big, even if you might fail. The trying is everything."

Miss Ida cleared her throat. "Well, I should see to the cleaning up, I suppose." She pushed back her chair and began to clear the table.

"Hold on, Miss Ida," Christy said. "You can't get away without telling us your dream."

"I don't have a dream," Miss Ida said primly. "Unless, of course, it's that someday Ruby Mae will finally learn to clean up her bedroom."

"Not so fast, Ida." David yanked on her apron string. "I admitted my dream. Fair is fair."

"I'm telling you, I don't have a dream," Miss Ida insisted. She pulled free of David's grasp and marched toward the kitchen. When she got to the door, she paused.

"Unless," she said, turning to look at the group with a little smile, "you count my secret dream to become a tap dancer." She demonstrated with a couple of quick steps, and vanished into the kitchen.

"Well, well," said Doctor MacNeill. "That's a side of Miss Ida we've never seen before!" He consulted his pocket watch. "I should be heading back to my cabin, folks. I want to make a stop on the way home and check on the Millers' new baby."

"Not so fast, Neil." Christy wagged her finger at him. "You're the only one who hasn't revealed a dream. We're not letting you escape that easily."

The doctor shrugged. "These days, I generally avoid dreaming. Real life is complicated enough. Seems to me having dreams just sets you up for failure."

"This, from a man who decided to practice medicine in such a remote corner of the world?" said Aunt Cora. "I'd call that quite a big dream."

"Come on," Ruby Mae urged, "just tell us one itty-bitty teensy-weensy dream. Ain't there somethin' you always wanted to learn yourself how to do? Like whittlin'?"

"Or playing the trombone?" Christy suggested.

23

"Or attending church regularly?" David added with a sly grin.

"Nope." Doctor MacNeill folded his arms over his chest. "Not a one."

"You're not leaving this table until you admit something," Christy warned.

The doctor rubbed his chin. "I can see I'm vastly outnumbered. All right. Maybe there is *one* thing. But you have to promise not to laugh. Especially you, Reverend."

"You have my solemn vow," David responded.

"I've always wanted to . . . well, learn how to paint. The mountains are so beautiful, I sometimes wish I could capture them on canvas forever." The doctor shook his head. "There. Now that I've made a complete fool of myself, are you all happy?"

"Neil, that's not the least bit foolish," Christy said gently. "I think it's a wonderful dream."

"And so do I," pronounced Aunt Cora. "Perhaps I'll send you some painting supplies when I get back to Knoxville."

"Oh, I wouldn't have the time," Doctor MacNeil said. "Don't bother, Aunt—"

"No bother. Who knows? We may have a budding artistic genius in our midst." She nudged Christy. "Not to mention a budding theatrical genius. Your play tomorrow could be the start of something wonderful."

"Well, it's a little smaller scale than the Knoxville Players. But it's the finest company of actors in the world."

≈ Four ≈

And now, I'd like everyone in our little theater company to take a final bow!"

It was the following afternoon. The play had been a wonderful success. Christy watched in delight as all of her students gathered at the front of the schoolroom. Everyone was there—the stagehands, the set decorators, the understudies, and the actors—even Little Burl, the curtain-puller.

The rest of the room was filled to capacity. Parents, grandparents, great-grandparents, younger sisters and brothers—it seemed as if everyone in Cutter Gap had shown up for the debut performance of *Goldilocks*. So many people had come, in fact, that many of them had been forced to watch the show through the windows.

Now they stood on their feet, applauding

and stomping and cheering and whistling. Christy held up her hand, and at her signal, all seventy students bowed, just the way she'd taught them. Slowly, Little Burl tugged the curtain across the stage.

"I want to thank you all for coming to our first performance," Christy called, but the audience was still applauding wildly and she could barely make herself heard.

She slipped behind the curtain. "Wonderful job, everybody!" she said to the excited students. She could see the pride shining in their eyes.

"They's still a-clappin' and carryin' on, Teacher," Creed exclaimed. "Ain't it a wonder?"

"They're clapping so hard because you deserve it," Christy said. "You know, I think that after all this excitement, I'm going to go ahead and dismiss class for the day. You all can head on out and find your families. Congratulations, everyone, on a wonderful performance!"

A few minutes later, David, Aunt Cora, and Doctor MacNeill made their way through the crowd to congratulate Christy.

"What a turnout!" David exclaimed. "And they were hanging on every word. I wish I could get these people to pay as close attention to my sermons!"

"Maybe if you dressed up in a bear costume, Reverend," Doctor MacNeill joked.

"You did a wonderful job, Christy," Aunt Cora said. "Those children just lit up the stage."

"I'm so proud of them," Christy said. "Especially children like Mountie O'Teale, the one who played Baby Bear. She's always been very shy around people. For a long time she even refused to speak. But there she was, out on that little stage, saying her lines like an old acting pro!"

"Christy," Aunt Cora said, "there's something I'd like to discuss with you." She exchanged a glance with Doctor MacNeill. "Please feel free to say no if you're not interested. I mean, I know how busy you are here with the school, and the timing isn't the best . . ."

"What is it?" Christy asked.

"Well, as I told you, our production of *Romeo and Juliet* begins soon. Because I'd planned this trip for so long, I left the play in the capable hands of my assistant director. Still, when I get back to Knoxville, there'll be plenty of last-minute chaos to contend with. I was wondering if you'd like to come back with me and help out with the production. I might even be able to get you a small part in the play."

Christy just stared in disbelief. She couldn't be quite sure, but she had the feeling that her mouth was hanging open.

"Christy," Doctor MacNeill elbowed her, "you're in distinct danger of drooling."

"I . . . I don't know what to say," Christy managed. "I mean, I'm so flattered that you asked, Aunt Cora. And it would be such an honor to help you. But I have my obligations here. The children, my work . . . I just couldn't . . ."

"Ah, but we're way ahead of you," said Doctor MacNeill. "The Reverend and Miss Alice have already agreed to take over your teaching duties while you're gone."

"Go on, Christy," David urged. "It'd do you good. Miss Alice and I can handle things just fine."

"I might even go along with you," said Doctor MacNeill. "I've got some friends in Knoxville—doctors I went to school with. And I'd love to spend more time with Aunt Cora."

"But I couldn't begin to afford a ticket—"

"It's my treat," Aunt Cora interrupted. "You'd be doing me a favor, actually. I'd welcome your help. It's the first rule of the theater: the last few days before a play debuts, things always seem to go wrong."

Christy hesitated. "But my going would be so silly, really. I'm not an actress. I'm not a director. I'm a teacher."

"It's a once-in-a-lifetime chance, Christy," said Doctor MacNeill. "You can't pass it up. It's your dream."

"I—I'll think about it," Christy stuttered. "Would that be all right, Aunt Cora?"

"Of course." Aunt Cora patted Christy on the shoulder. "You take all the time you need. But remember this line from Shakespeare, dear:

Our doubts are traitors,
And make us lose the good we oft might win,
By fearing to attempt.

Doctor MacNeill grinned. "Translation—what have you got to lose?"

"Nothing, I suppose . . ." Christy said. Under her breath she added, "except my pride."

I just don't know what to do, Miss Alice."

A week had passed, and Christy still hadn't made up her mind about Aunt Cora's offer. This afternoon, after school had let out, Christy had come to Miss Alice's cabin, hoping to get some much-needed advice.

"I have to decide something soon," Christy said. "Aunt Cora's going back to Knoxville in two days."

Miss Alice, dressed in a crisp dark green linen skirt and white blouse, was brewing tea. She turned to Christy, smiling. "Try looking at things this way. What's the worse thing that could happen if you went on this little adventure?"

Christy sank into a rocking chair. "The worst thing? Well, I'd be abandoning my students. They might lose ground on their spelling and grammar work. And I'm just starting to get some discipline in my classroom. That could all go down the drain."

"In a few days' time? Don't you think David and I are competent to handle things?"

"Of course," Christy said quickly. "I suppose I'm just feeling guilty about leaving my students. Even if it is for just a little while."

Miss Alice poured steaming tea into two china teacups painted with dainty pink roses. She handed one to Christy, then sat beside her. "Well, what else could go wrong? Let's look a little deeper."

"Well, I could just get in Aunt Cora's way, for one thing. I doubt she really needs my help. She's just being kind."

"What makes you say that?"

"I don't know the first thing about the theater, not really. Not like she does."

"I'm sure you could help out in any number of ways," Miss Alice argued. "And besides, you have had some experience in the theater."

"That was in high school, Miss Alice—not professional theater!" Christy sipped the hot peppermint tea. "Or were you referring to my directing debut at the Cutter Gap Community Theater?"

Miss Alice laughed. "Everyone has to start somewhere."

"Suppose I did go to Knoxville," Christy said, "and I actually managed to land a role on stage. I'm sure I'd end up tripping on my skirt or forgetting my lines. Just imagine how embarrassing *that* would be!"

"So the worst thing you can imagine is that you might trip on stage, in front of hundreds of people?"

"Well, it *would* be pretty humiliating, don't you think?" Christy cried.

"Being embarrassed is part of being human, Christy. We all make mistakes. We all try things and fail. The important thing is that we do try—and keep trying. That's what God wants from us. That we try. That we do our best. He doesn't expect perfection."

"I know. But still . . ." Christy's voice trailed off.

"Do you recall when you first came here to teach?" Miss Alice asked. "Remember how discouraged you were, faced with such a huge class? I told you a story about a baby."

Christy nodded. "It was about a baby learning to walk. How he wobbles and falls and maybe even bumps his nose. But he just gets up and tries again. He doesn't care what anybody thinks. All he cares about is learning to walk. Oh yes, I remember." She gave a laugh. "You're saying if I fall on my fanny in front of hundreds of people, I should just brush myself off like that baby and try again?"

"That's exactly what I'm saying. As I told

you before, we Quakers like to say that all discouragement is from an evil source, and that it can only end in more evil. The important thing is that you will have tried something new and difficult. And you will have learned and grown as a person. That's all that matters."

Christy gazed out the bank of windows across the back of the room. It was a breathtaking view. The towering peaks and lush greenery spread out before them like a gigantic painting. No wonder the doctor wished he could capture a scene like this on canvas.

She wondered if he would ever try his hand at painting. Probably not. He was too proud, too afraid to fail at something he thought was "silly."

Christy pursed her lips. "Are you absolutely sure that you and David can handle things?"

"Absolutely and positively."

"All right, then." Christy set down her teacup and leapt to her feet. "I'm going to give it a try. I may look foolish. But I'm going to do it!"

"Wonderful!"

Christy's hand flew to her mouth. "I haven't even started packing! And I've got to put lesson plans together, and tell Aunt Cora, and . . . oh, dear, Miss Alice! I've got to go!"

"Can't you even finish your tea?"

"I don't think so. I'm too excited."

Miss Alice watched, grinning, as Christy raced for the door. "Christy?" she called.

"Yes?"

"I was going to say 'break a leg.' After all, it's an expression of good luck in the theater. But I'm afraid you're so frantic, you might just take me literally."

"How about giving me a hug instead?" Christy asked, rushing to her side.

"Even better," Miss Alice agreed.

⚛ Six ⚛

I can't believe I'm really on this train," Christy whispered. "I'm not dreaming this, am I?"

Doctor MacNeill pinched his arm. "No. I seem to be quite awake. I definitely felt that. How about you, Aunt Cora?"

Aunt Cora was seated across from the doctor and Christy on the red velvet seat. "I'm happy to report I'm quite awake," she said.

They had spent the previous afternoon traveling from Cutter Gap to the small town of El Pano. There, they'd spent the night at a boardinghouse. Christy had stayed there on her first trip to Cutter Gap months earlier. Now, at last, they were on their way to Knoxville.

"My, my," Aunt Cora said, her head cocked to one side.

"What?" the doctor asked.

"Has anyone ever told you two you make a rather handsome couple?"

Christy felt certain she'd turned as red as the cushions. But Doctor MacNeill just winked. "I think what you have here is more like the pairing of Beauty and the Beast, Aunt Cora."

"Neil's just being modest," Christy whispered to Aunt Cora.

Christy lay back against the cushion and watched the deep green forests flash past. Riding in this train reminded her of her trip to Tennessee several months ago to begin her work in Cutter Gap.

The smells and sights and sounds were so familiar! The scent of coal dust in the railroad car. The brass spittoons. The potbellied stove in the rear. The sacks of grain and produce piled toward the back. And, of course, the shrill whistle of the train.

The car rocked gently back and forth. The steady click-click-click of the wheels was deeply soothing. Christy's eyelids were heavy, but she didn't want to sleep. She couldn't let herself miss a moment of this adventure.

In the window glass, she caught sight of her reflection. Again she was reminded of that cold day last January. That's when she'd left her parents' home in Asheville to teach school at the Cutter Gap Mission in the Smoky Mountains. She was wearing the same fawn-colored coatsuit, but she had changed in many other ways. Her hair was longer now and streaked by the sun. Her skin was bronzed. Her hands were calloused from working in Miss Ida's garden. She looked older than her nineteen years, and maybe even a little bit wiser.

She'd been so afraid that January day! And she'd felt so very alone. Now, here she was, seated next to two good friends, with so many more back home in Cutter Gap. Perhaps that was the most important—and the most wonderful—change of all.

Christy reached into her satchel and pulled out her diary. "Are you taking notes?" Aunt Cora inquired.

"This is my diary. I started it when I left Asheville to teach in Cutter Gap."

Christy opened to the first page. There, in her pretty, flowing handwriting, was the entry she'd made her first day:

The truth is, I have not been this afraid before, or felt this alone and homesick. Leaving everyone I love was harder than I thought it would be. But I must be strong. I am at the start of a great adventure. And great adventures are sometimes scary.

Doctor MacNeill peeked over Christy's arm.

"I'll bet that's interesting reading. Do I make an appearance?"

Christy slapped the little book shut. "You're as bad as George." She winked at Aunt Cora. "That's my younger brother. I used to keep my old diary under lock and key to prevent him from sneaking a peek at it. Once he actually managed to open it with a screwdriver. Fortunately, I caught him just in the nick of time." She pointed her finger at the doctor. "Trespassers will be prosecuted to the full extent of the law, Neil."

He held up his hands in a gesture of surrender. "Fine, fine. I guess I'll just have to take a nap instead."

He leaned back against the seat and closed his eyes. Aunt Cora opened up her book of Shakespeare's plays and began to read. Confident she could write in privacy, Christy got out her pen and began to write. The jiggling railroad car made it difficult to be neat, but she did the best she could:

I'm on another adventure! And I'm almost as nervous as I was the day I headed to Cutter Gap on that train, pulled by the engine everyone called "Old Buncombe."

Of course, this time I know there's not so much at stake. As Miss Alice pointed out, I have nothing to lose but some dignity. And who knows what I might learn from this experience?

As we were leaving Cutter Gap, Miss Alice whispered something in my ear, a favorite Bible quote of hers: "He which soweth bountifully shall reap also bountifully."

I think what she was trying to tell me was that there is no telling what I might gain from taking this risk.

But fear is a funny thing. I feel excited and nervous all the way down to my toes. My stomach's doing flip-flops. I'm still hours away from Knoxville, and nowhere near that big theater where I may actually make my big-city debut.

I know the worst that can happen—I'll end up a little humbler. That wouldn't be such a bad thing, would it? Still and all, it would be awfully nice if I could shake this feeling that I'm getting in way over my head.

Christy closed up her diary and tucked it into her satchel. Telephone poles flew past outside her window.

Doctor MacNeill opened one eye. "Done writing?"

"For now, anyway."

He smiled. "I sure would like to know what's in that diary of yours. It's tantalizing, knowing that the secrets of your heart are only a few inches away."

"If you want to read a diary, you'll have to get one of your own, Neil."

"Now, *that* would be some boring reading,"

he replied. "Try to get some sleep. It's a long trip."

"How can you sleep? I'm too excited—and nervous."

"Nervous?" Doctor MacNeill asked. "What's there to be nervous about?"

Christy grinned. "Nothing, I hope. But I guess I'll find out soon enough."

❧ Seven ❧

Look out, Aunt Cora!" Christy cried, for what had to be the dozenth time.

Aunt Cora braked her car in the nick of time, narrowly avoiding a man pulling a mule and a small cart. "Whoopsie," she said with a smile.

It was early evening when they arrived at the train station in Knoxville. Aunt Cora had insisted on driving home. She'd left her old car parked in the street, right in front of the station. Doctor MacNeill had offered to drive, but Aunt Cora wouldn't hear of it.

"Nonsense. You haven't driven since you were in medical school, and then it was just when your friend Peter Mulberry would lend you his old rattletrap," Aunt Cora had said firmly. "And it's not like you have the opportunity to drive much in Cutter Gap, Neil.

Trust me. Ever since your Uncle Robert died, I've taken care of all the driving. And I'm a natural, if I do say so myself."

Now, after several minutes of lurching stops and breathtaking turns, Christy wasn't so sure. Aunt Cora was so busy pointing out the sights that she often lost track of the road.

"And over there—see that little white clapboard church? That's where Neil's Uncle Robert and I were married."

"It's lovely, Aunt Cora," Christy replied, gripping the seat till her knuckles were white. "By the way, I think you were supposed to stop back there—"

"Pish. I checked. Didn't see a thing." Aunt Cora pointed out the window with her gloved hand. "And that park over there? That's where Neil and his cousin Lucy used to play when they came to visit us in the summer. Remember, Neil? You were cute as a button—"

"Aunt Cora?" The doctor cleared his throat. "I think that fruit truck was honking at us."

"People can be so rude!" she muttered.

Finally, to Christy's great relief, Aunt Cora stopped the car in the driveway of a lovely, white brick home.

Sitting in a rocker on the porch was a thin, balding man with wire-rimmed spectacles. He was bent over, elbows on his knees, hands cupping his chin. He looked very forlorn.

"Oh my," Aunt Cora whispered. "It's Oliver. This doesn't look good at all—not at all."

"Who's Oliver?" asked Doctor MacNeill.

Aunt Cora waved at the man, who simply gave a sullen nod.

"Oliver Flump," she explained, "is the assistant director of the Knoxville Players. He's a very nice man, but he tends to get a little . . . well, *flustered* sometimes. The slightest little thing will set him into a tizzy. I left him in charge of the play in the hope it would boost his self-confidence."

"He doesn't look very self-confident," Christy said.

"No, indeed he doesn't. Well—" Aunt Cora flung open the car door, "I suppose we might as well see what the problem is. I'm sure it's nothing. It usually is."

While the doctor retrieved their bags, Christy and Aunt Cora joined Oliver on the porch.

"Mr. Oliver Flump, I'd like you to meet Miss Christy Huddleston of Cutter Gap, Tennessee."

"How do you do, Miss Huddleston?" Oliver said. He had a mournful, high voice. It reminded Christy of one of Jeb Spencer's hound dogs, whining for supper.

"It's nice to meet you, Mr. Flump."

"Please, call me Oliver. Everybody does."

"Are you just here as a one-man welcoming committee, Oliver?" Aunt Cora asked. She held open the front door. Christy headed inside, followed by a slouching Oliver. "Or has something gone wrong with the play?"

Oliver went straight to the parlor and dropped into an overstuffed chair. He groaned. "It's too awful to say out loud. My career in the theater is doomed. That's all I have to say on the subject. One word— *doomed*."

"That's what you said when we did our last play. And the play before that, as I recall," said Aunt Cora. "Christy, come. Help me light the lamps while Oliver recounts his tale of woe."

"This time it's no laughing matter, Cora," Oliver said defensively.

"What have I told you about that hangdog attitude, Oliver?" Aunt Cora asked cheerfully as she lit a lamp near the mantel. "How will anyone else ever believe in Oliver Flump, if he doesn't believe in himself?"

Christy lit a lamp on a walnut table next to Oliver. "You have a lovely home, Aunt Cora."

"Why, thank you, Christy. See the framed theater programs on the wall? Those are from my days in New York City. I was much younger then—thinner, too—" she added with a chuckle. "I must have seen every show I could afford, and more I couldn't. Sometimes I just got the inexpensive seats up in the balcony. Oh, but the plays I saw performed! All of Shakespeare's comedies, and most of his tragedies! Oh, my—" she put her hand to her heart, "what days those were!"

Doctor MacNeill entered, carrying the bags. "Shall I put these upstairs?"

"No, no. Come sit a spell. We'll make a fire in the fireplace, and Oliver will tell us his tale of woe. Oliver, meet my nephew, Doctor Neil MacNeill. Finest physician in the entire United States. I'd say the whole world, but I don't want to sound like a boastful relative."

The doctor shook Oliver's hand. "I understand you're Aunt Cora's right-hand man."

"No longer. Not after all that's happened." Oliver sighed. "I'm doomed, you see—and so is our play."

Aunt Cora clucked her tongue. "Oliver, dear. Please tell me what's wrong, without any dramatics." She sat down on the couch across from him. "I'm sure we can make a quick fix of it. You know you have a tendency to over-react."

"I most certainly do not!" Oliver cried.

"Remember the posters for *The Taming of the Shrew*? Remember how you offered to resign over them? Three times, as I recall."

"That was a definite crisis," Oliver explained to Christy and the doctor. "You see, they'd printed them wrong. The posters read '*The*

46

Taming of the Shoe.' Who, I ask you, wants to see a play about a shoe?"

"At least it was a tame shoe," Aunt Cora said lightly, "and not one of those wild, ferocious, man-eating shoes."

"It wasn't funny, Cora." Oliver rubbed his eyes. "It was a nightmare—a true nightmare."

"Nonsense," Aunt Cora said. "We all got a good laugh out of it."

"Well, try getting a laugh out of this," Oliver said bitterly. "Sarah McGeorge has laryngitis. She can't even whisper her lines."

"No problem. Pansy Trotman will make a fine Juliet," Aunt Cora said with a wave of her hand. "She's Sarah's understudy," she explained.

Oliver folded his arms over his chest. "And as if that weren't enough, the entire theater company is threatening to quit unless *I* quit!"

"Oh, my," said Aunt Cora. "That is a bit of a pickle, I must admit. Have you been short with them, Oliver? You know you can be rather demanding."

"I have most certainly not been short with them," Oliver replied. "In fact, I've exhibited saintly patience, despite their insults and belligerence."

"Well, I'll have a little talk with them. We'll work things out."

"It's too late." Oliver sighed. "I'm resigning.

47

The production is yours. The truth is, I'm glad to be done with it. This play is doomed."

❧ Eight ❧

There it is," Aunt Cora said the next morning, "my home away from home. Isn't it beautiful?"

Christy gazed at the ornate brass doors of the theater. A large poster at the ticket window announced the upcoming production of *Romeo and Juliet*. In the bright sun, the whole building seemed to shimmer.

"I can't believe we're really here," she whispered.

"We're here, all right." Aunt Cora swung open the doors. "Come on. I'll introduce you and Neil to all the gang."

Christy and the doctor followed Aunt Cora through the silent, empty lobby. An oriental carpet covered the floor. Posters from other performances hung on the walls.

Aunt Cora led them to another set of doors. "Hear that yelling in there?" she asked. "Welcome to the glamorous world of the theater!"

Doctor MacNeill opened the doors. Christy gasped. There, spread before her, was the theater of her dreams—the hundreds of seats, the broad stage, the thick velvet curtains. Everything was just as she'd imagined it.

On the stage, a large group of people hurried to and fro. Some were carrying pages, reciting lines to themselves. Some had paint cans or brushes. A young boy was hammering away at a wooden set.

In the center of all the turmoil was a familiar face. "Isn't that Oliver?" Christy asked.

"I knew he wouldn't really resign," said Aunt Cora. "He never does. He loves the theater as much as I do."

"I am *not* overacting," a young man cried from the stage. "I am emoting! I am having emotions, Oliver! You, on the other hand, are not directing! You are *dictating*!"

Aunt Cora hustled down the aisle, clapping her hands to get attention. Christy smiled. It reminded her of her own attempt at directing seventy schoolchildren.

"People, please!" Aunt Cora yelled. "Let's have a little civility! We have guests!" She crooked a finger. "Christy, Neil, come sit down here. You can have front-row seats today. Tomorrow I'll really put you to work, Christy."

"Cora's back!" somebody yelled, and the people on stage broke into applause.

"Thank goodness!" someone else said. "The reign of terror is over!"

Oliver threw up his hands. "See, Cora? Do you see what I've had to put up with in your absence?"

"You!" cried a dark-haired woman in a purple silk dress. She raced to the edge of the stage. "Cora, Oliver has been a tyrant! An absolute tyrant! He's been changing my set designs, belittling the actors, and nit-picking over every little detail! He's been impossible. What a relief it is to have you back!"

"Now, now. Let's everyone settle down." Aunt Cora took a seat next to Christy. "As I told you all before, Oliver is in charge of this production. I am here to offer advice and hold hands and dry tears. But in the end, Oliver is the boss."

"Then I quit!" the woman shouted.

"Me too!" someone else cried.

"You can't quit," Oliver said, "because I'm quitting first!"

"You already quit," said the dark-haired woman. "But here you are, back again, like a bad penny."

A young man with curly brown hair and the wide, innocent eyes of a fawn stepped forward. "It's like this, Cora," he said calmly. "We just can't work with Oliver, not when he's in charge." He cast an apologetic glance at Oliver. "He just plain gets too upset. And when he gets upset, I get upset. And when I get upset, well . . . I can't remember my lines, no matter how hard I try." He shoved his hands in his pockets and shrugged. "I guess what I'm saying is, if Oliver stays, I have to go. That means you will have lost your Romeo *and* your Juliet. Although, of course, the understudies could handle things just fine." He shrugged again. "Anyway, that's my two-cents' worth."

Aunt Cora hesitated. "Oliver, what should we do about this situation? The cast seems to think you've been rather demanding."

"They're prima donnas, all of them," Oliver sniffed. "They don't realize that pain is the price of perfection."

"One thing I've learned from this job, Oliver," said Aunt Cora, "perfectionism can get in the way of having a good time. Suppose you and I direct this production together? Share the power, as it were? Maybe next time you can take a whack at running the show yourself."

Oliver's shoulders slumped. "It's no use. I tried to give it another shot, but clearly, if I'm not wanted . . ."

"Of course you're wanted," Aunt Cora soothed.

"No, he isn't," snapped the dark-haired woman.

"Fine. Then I quit—for real this time," Oliver cried. With that, he stomped off stage and disappeared.

"Arabella," Aunt Cora said, "you didn't have to be so cruel."

"I wasn't being cruel—just truthful," Arabella said. "Oliver's fine as an assistant director, Cora. But whenever you put him in charge, he goes mad with the power."

Aunt Cora climbed the steps to the stage. "Well, I guess the important thing to do right now is get down to business. First of all, I want to introduce you to Miss Christy Huddleston and Doctor Neil MacNeill. Both are from Cutter Gap, Tennessee. Some of you may already have met Neil, my nephew. Miss Huddleston is a budding actress and director in her own right, in addition to being a fine teacher. She's here to help out with the production, and perhaps take a walk-on role."

Arabella cleared her throat loudly. "Speaking of roles, Cora. Now that Sarah's lost her voice, I really think I'm perfect to step into the role of Juliet."

"Arabella, we've been through this already. You're the set and costume designer. Not an actress. Besides, we have a wonderful Juliet at the ready, in the person of Pansy Trotman, her understudy."

"But I'd be perfect for the role," Arabella argued. "Just watch."

Arabella put her hand to her heart, sighed, and crumpled to the ground in a heap.

"Arabella, I've seen your crumple before. You are an excellent crumpler. But the part belongs to Pansy." Aunt Cora turned to Christy and the doctor. "The excellent crumpling you've just witnessed was performed by none other than our own Miss Arabella Devaine. She's been designing costumes and sets for us for years."

Arabella got to her feet, clearly pouting.

"That handsome young man over there is Mr. Gilroy Gannon, our fine Romeo," Aunt Cora continued.

Gilroy, the curly-haired man who'd spoken earlier, waved to Christy and Doctor MacNeill.

"Over there is Miss Pansy Trotman, our new Juliet. And painting away on the balcony set back in the corner are Miss Marylou Marsh and her brother Vernon."

The pretty girl with the paintbrush gave a nod. She was thin, with long blond hair and a shy smile.

"Marylou?" Doctor MacNeill asked. "Is that really you?"

Marylou took a few steps forward. Her smile broadened. "Hi, Neil. You look different too. As I recall, you were rather scrawny."

"I met Marylou one summer when I came here to visit Aunt Cora," the doctor explained to Christy.

"Well, I should get back to my painting," Marylou said softly.

"We'll have to get together and talk over old times," the doctor said.

"That's an excellent suggestion!" exclaimed Aunt Cora. "Listen up, everyone! I've just decided to have a party at my home tomorrow evening. We'll call it an early cast party. That way my nephew and Miss Huddleston can get to know everyone. You're all invited, and I expect you all to come!"

"Already she's giving orders," Gilroy said with a smile. "You're as bad as Oliver, Cora."

"No one's as bad as Oliver," Arabella muttered.

"Enough of this," Aunt Cora said. "We're here to rehearse, not complain. Let us begin, as they say, at the beginning. Act one, scene one! Places, everyone!"

❧ Nine ❧

So, Christy," Aunt Cora said at the party the following evening, "what do you think of theater life so far? You've been with us for two days now."

"I think," Christy replied, "it's a lot more like a schoolroom full of unruly children than I'd ever imagined."

Aunt Cora laughed. "Dear, you've hit the nail right on the head!"

The party had been a wonderful success. Aunt Cora's home was filled to overflowing with the cast and crew. After dinner, some of the stagehands had moved Aunt Cora's furniture into the corners so that people could dance. Three musicians had brought their instruments along, and now they were playing a lilting waltz.

Christy already felt as if she knew most of

the cast. Gilroy was the shy, clumsy, loveable Romeo. Pansy was the sweet understudy who was now playing the role of Juliet, so emotional she could instantly cry on cue. Arabella was the sharp-tongued designer. Oliver was the assistant director with a flair for the dramatic.

"I'm surprised Oliver came tonight," Christy whispered to Aunt Cora. They were standing near the fireplace, watching the others come and go.

"I'm not. Oliver loves us all, and we love him, in spite of all the complaining. He's still nursing a grudge, though. You'll notice how he's hovering in a corner, looking forlorn and resentful."

"I haven't seen Pansy tonight," Christy said.

"Nor have I," said Aunt Cora. "She seemed rather distracted today. Perhaps it's the strain of taking on the lead role."

Christy nodded. "That would be enough to make anyone distracted!"

"My, isn't that Marylou that Neil's dancing with?" Aunt Cora asked. "He's quite light on his feet, isn't he?"

"Were they . . . good friends?" Christy asked, trying very hard not to sound jealous.

"Very good," Aunt Cora replied.

As the waltz came to an end, Christy couldn't help wondering just what *very good* meant. Was it possible that Neil and Marylou had been sweethearts once upon a time?

She watched as the doctor bowed politely to Marylou. He paused at the refreshment table, then strode over, munching on a cookie. "You ladies look lovely this evening."

"And you looked lovely on the dance floor," Christy said, a bit frostily.

"You're too kind, Christy. After all, you've had the painful experience of dancing with me."

"What did you do today, while we were at the theater?" Aunt Cora asked. "I do hope you haven't been too bored, dear."

"Nope. Looked up ol' James Briley. He's that old friend of mine from medical school, Christy. The one who invited me to come to Knoxville to work a while back?"

"I take it you said no?" Aunt Cora asked.

"I was sorely tempted," Doctor MacNeill admitted. "But in the end, Christy helped me see that I belonged in Cutter Gap."

"My loss," Aunt Cora said with a sigh. "But Cutter Gap's gain. In any case, you're always welcome to join us at the theater. Or perhaps we could get you started on those art lessons you've always wanted. I've got a neighbor who's a wonderful artist. I'm sure she'd be delighted to teach you the basics while you're here."

Doctor MacNeill laughed. "I'll find something less challenging to do with my time, Aunt Cora!"

The musicians began a new waltz. "Would either of you ladies care to dance?" Doctor MacNeill asked.

For a moment Christy hesitated. "I'd be honored," she replied at last.

It was difficult dancing in such crowded quarters, but somehow everyone managed. Christy and the doctor swept around the room in tight circles, spinning to the lilting music.

"Having fun so far?" the doctor asked.

"Oh, yes."

"Glad you decided to come?"

"Absolutely," Christy replied.

"By the way, I have a feeling Romeo has a long-distance crush on you," the doctor said. "I've noticed him watching you from afar."

"Gilroy?" Christy cried. "He's hardly said two words to me. But speaking of crushes, I noticed Marylou is over by the piano, sneaking rather dreamy-eyed peeks at you. Maybe you should ask her for another dance, Neil." She gave him a rather shy look. "After all, you said you two were old friends."

"I'm not sure 'friends' is quite the right word," the doctor said with a wry grin. "Marylou used to beat me up on a regular basis."

"Marylou? That sweet, tiny thing? Used to beat *you* up?"

The doctor nodded. "Pummeled me into the ground on a regular basis."

Christy couldn't help laughing. "But why?"

"I couldn't tell you. You know how children are. But it was very humiliating. I couldn't fight back, because, of course, my mother had taught me never to hit a girl."

"Come to think of it, I did hear Marylou ask if you ever learned to fight back. It sounds to me like you could have been too scrawny and weak to fight back. Are you sure you *could* have fought back?"

The doctor rolled his eyes. "It's a good thing this waltz is coming to an end. I can see where this conversation is going. You're never going to let me live this down, are you?"

Just as Christy started to respond, Arabella came rushing into the room.

"I have terrible news!" Arabella cried. "The most dreadful, terrible news!"

Everyone fell silent. Arabella ran to Aunt Cora's side. "Come, Cora. I think you should be sitting down when you hear this."

Aunt Cora shook her off impatiently. "Goodness, Arabella! Will you just tell me what's happened? Has someone died?"

"She might as well have." Arabella fanned her face with her hand, as if she were in danger of fainting. "It's Pansy."

"Pansy? What's happened to Pansy?" Aunt Cora demanded.

Arabella paused, glancing around the room to be sure she had everyone's attention. "When dear little Pansy didn't show up for the party, I felt compelled to call her at home to be sure she was well. After all, you know how Pansy loves a party."

"The point, Arabella," Aunt Cora grumbled. "Get to the point."

"Well, her mother answered, and she was positively beside herself, poor woman. Of course, who could blame her? I mean, if Pansy were *my* daughter. . . . Not, mind you, that I'm old enough to have a daughter Pansy's age, but still—"

"The point, Arabella!" Aunt Cora cried.

Arabella took a long, dramatic pause. "Pansy," she said softly, "has eloped!"

"Eloped!" Aunt Cora cried. "With whom?"

"The butcher on Pine Street. You know the one. Mustache, big ears? A nice enough man, but still . . ."

"I *told* you this play was doomed!" Oliver declared triumphantly. "And now you have the proof. Juliet number one loses her voice. And now Juliet number two runs off with a butcher, without so much as a proper farewell! If that's not doomed, I don't know what is! We are officially Juliet-less!"

"Settle down, Oliver. I'm sure we'll think of

something," Aunt Cora said. Still, for the first time since Christy had met her, Aunt Cora looked genuinely worried.

"Speaking as Romeo, this is very hard to take," Gilroy said. "I can't keep falling madly in love with a new Juliet every other day." He sighed. "It's much too confusing."

"How are we ever going to find another Juliet on such short notice?" Aunt Cora asked.

"Look no further, Cora," said Arabella. "*I* shall rescue us from the jaws of defeat. It will be a terrible sacrifice, to be sure—long hours, terrific pressure, even the jealousy of my peers. But through it all, one guiding philosophy will sustain me." She clasped her hands together. "The show, my dear friends, must go on!"

Aunt Cora thoughtfully considered the situation. "That's a fine offer, Arabella. One might even say a noble sacrifice. However, I have just one question for you. Do you know the part?"

"Do I know the part? Do *I* know the part?" Arabella cried. "Just listen!"

She dropped to her knees while the others stared. "O Romeo, Romeo, wherefore art thou Romeo?"

Arabella paused. She looked around the room, biting her lip. "Um, the rest slips my mind for the moment. I think it's something about love."

"That's a pretty safe guess," the doctor whispered to Christy.

"Arabella," Aunt Cora said patiently, "I know how much you want this part, dear. And maybe, if we had more time to prepare you. . . . But right now, we need someone who already knows all the lines. Someone who can learn the staging quickly, and be ready to go on opening night."

Arabella jumped to her feet. "And where exactly are you ever going to find someone like that?" she demanded.

It was a good question, Christy thought. A very good question.

Suddenly, she realized Aunt Cora was staring directly at her.

So was Doctor MacNeill.

And she had a very good idea what they were both thinking.

Christy!" Aunt Cora exclaimed.

"Christy," Doctor MacNeill said.

"Christy?" Oliver asked.

"Christy!" Gilroy cried.

"Christy?" Arabella screamed.

Christy took a step backward. All eyes were on her.

Aunt Cora looked hopeful. Doctor MacNeill looked encouraging. Oliver looked doubtful. Gilroy looked happy. Arabella looked shocked.

"Christy has performed the role of Juliet on stage," Aunt Cora said.

"In a high school gymnasium, Aunt Cora," Christy added quickly, "not on a real, professional stage."

"What's the difference?" Aunt Cora said. "An audience is an audience."

"B-but it was just an amateur production,"

Christy argued. "Halfway through the balcony scene, Romeo's little brother, Harry, jumped out of the audience, climbed onstage, and joined me in the balcony."

"And what did you do when Harry showed up?" Aunt Cora asked.

"I made up an extra line. I told Romeo I had to go because it was past my little brother's bedtime."

"The mark of a true professional!" Aunt Cora said. "The theater is always full of surprises. That's one of the reasons we love it so."

"I think Christy would make a lovely Juliet," Gilroy said.

"Told you he has a crush on you," the doctor whispered to Christy.

"But she's from Cutter Gap!" Arabella objected.

"So?" asked Gilroy.

"Well, we're the *Knoxville* Players, Gilroy."

Gilroy groaned. "I was born in Virginia, Arabella. This isn't about where you're from. It's about finding someone who can do the job."

"Gilroy is right," Aunt Cora agreed. "There are plenty of people in this room who know *some* of Juliet's lines. But there's only one person in this room who knows *all* of them."

"It isn't fair," Arabella pouted.

"Life isn't always fair, Arabella," Aunt Cora

said. "And speaking of fair, we haven't even asked Christy how she feels about all this."

A long pause followed. Everyone was waiting for Christy to respond. She tried to answer, but her mouth refused to make a sound.

See? a voice inside of her taunted. *You're tongue-tied in front of these people, Christy. It was one thing to play Juliet in front of your friends and family. It's quite another to perform in front of strangers in a professional theater.*

"I-I couldn't," Christy stuttered at last. "I mean, I'd love to help, I really would. But I just couldn't. I could do a walk-on part, maybe—one without any lines. I couldn't play Juliet."

"Christy, at least think about it," Aunt Cora began, but Christy didn't need to think about it. Her mind was made up. She quietly excused herself and went upstairs.

Behind her, she could hear Oliver's sad pronouncement: "I *told* you this play was doomed."

— ～ —

Later that evening, there was a firm knock at Christy's bedroom door. "Christy? It's Neil. Did you find the party too boring?"

"It certainly wasn't boring." Christy opened the door.

The doctor leaned against the door jamb, arms crossed over his chest. "Everyone was sorry to see you go."

"Sorry," Christy shrugged. "I didn't know what else to do. I hated to let them all down, but I just can't do it, Neil. I was nervous enough about coming here and helping out in some small way. I didn't expect to be forced to take the starring role in a play."

"I understand. Aunt Cora said they may just cancel the play for the time being."

"Is she all right?"

"Oh, sure. She's a little disappointed, maybe." The doctor chuckled. "She's not as disappointed as Arabella, certainly."

Christy sighed. "Aunt Cora would be even more disappointed if I went out on stage, opened my mouth and nothing came out."

"Personally, I've never found you to be short of words."

"You don't understand. I don't even know if I remember all the lines, Neil! It's been a long time. And how do I know I wouldn't freeze up in front of all those people? Just stand there like a stone statue?"

"You don't. I guess you won't ever know unless you try." The doctor thought for a moment. "Seems to me you have to ask yourself if you'll look back on this moment someday and regret not having taken advantage of the opportunity. At least, that's what

67

Aunt Cora told me tonight, after I refused her offer of art lessons again."

"Why don't you try your hand at painting, Neil? If Aunt Cora knows a good teacher, this would be the perfect chance for you. It'd be a shame to pass it up . . ." Christy's voice trailed off. "I guess that sounds kind of silly coming from me, doesn't it?"

"I'll make you a deal," the doctor said. "I'll try my hand at painting, if you'll try your hand at playing Juliet. Just a day or two. No commitment."

Christy didn't answer. Her heart felt as if it were in her throat. She walked over to the window. Stars were scattered across the night sky, like glittering wildflowers in a field of endless black. Back home in Cutter Gap, her students might be looking up at this very sky right now—mischievous Creed, or gentle Little Burl, or fast-talking Ruby Mae.

What would they say, if she went back and told them about her adventure in Knoxville? How would they react, knowing their teacher had been too afraid to take a chance?

"You came all this way, Christy," the doctor said, joining her at the window, "Don't give up now."

Christy turned to him. "All right, then," she said at last, "but I want you to promise me something."

"Anything."

"If you get to see me perform as Juliet, then I get to see your very first painting."

"You drive a hard bargain, Christy Huddleston," the doctor said with a smile. He placed a soft kiss on her cheek. "It's a deal."

✤ Eleven ✤

All right," Aunt Cora announced the next morning at the theater, "first things first. As most of you have heard by now, Christy has agreed to take on the demanding role of Juliet. For that, we are all very grateful."

"Hmmph," someone muttered.

Aunt Cora shot a warning look in Arabella's direction.

"Don't look at me!" Arabella cried. "I wish her nothing but the best."

"I want you all to be on your best behavior for the next few days," Aunt Cora continued. "Help show Christy the ropes. Make her feel at home. We've got a lot of ground to cover, and not much time. Christy, here's a copy of the play for you to look over. Use it the first couple of days of rehearsal to refresh your memory."

"Thank you," Christy said softly. "And I just want to tell everybody I'm grateful for this chance, and I'll do the very best I can. But please don't expect too much."

"You'll do just great." Gilroy patted her on the back. "If you got any questions, I'm the guy to ask. After all—" he winked, "I am Romeo."

"Later, we'll do a wardrobe fitting," Arabella said, eyeing Christy up and down. "I'll probably have to let out the costumes a bit," she said with the hint of a sneer.

"Whenever you say, Arabella," Christy said meekly.

"All right, people!" Aunt Cora clapped her hands. "I want to start this morning with act two, scene one. Romeo, Benvolio, Mercutio, let's get started." She turned to Christy. "Why don't you find yourself a nice, quiet spot to look over your lines? And don't hesitate to ask if you need anything."

What I really need is a dose of courage, Christy thought as she headed backstage. She almost wished the doctor were there for moral support. But today he was starting his art lessons, just as he'd promised.

In any case, it would probably have just made her more nervous to have Doctor MacNeill there, watching her stumble over her lines. He'd get to see her fail soon enough, on opening night. Assuming, that is, she lasted that long.

Christy found a wooden bench behind some props in an out-of-the-way corner of the stage. She got out her copy of the play and began to read through her lines.

"Hi, there."

Christy turned to see Marylou approaching. She was dressed in her dirty, paint-spattered overalls. A sprinkle of sawdust covered her hair.

"Hi, Marylou. What have you been up to?"

"A little of everything." Marylou shrugged shyly. "Sometimes I help with sets. Sometimes I do things for Oliver, when he starts to go crazy. Mostly, I help Ara-bellow." She grinned. "Oops. That's what we call her behind her back sometimes. It isn't very nice, I know."

"I imagine she can be rather difficult to work with."

"You're right about that." Marylou sat down on another bench. "So. You're going to be Juliet. Are you excited?"

"Scared, more than anything. But after talking it over with Doctor MacNeill last night, I decided I owed it to myself to give it a shot."

"You and Neil, you're pretty close?" Marylou asked carefully. "I saw you dancing at the party."

"He's a good friend, yes."

"You aim to marry him?"

Christy blushed at Marylou's rather blunt question. "I don't know about that . . ."

"No need to say anything. I can tell by the way you're gettin' all red that you're a little sweet on him."

Christy hesitated. She could feel her face burning.

"I figured as much," Marylou said. "Neil . . . well, he's quite a catch." She leapt off the bench. "Well, I have to get going. Ara-bellow wants me to help her mend some costumes."

"See you later," Christy called as Marylou dashed off. *He's quite a catch,* Marylou's words echoed in Christy's mind. Just how well did Marylou know Doctor MacNeill, anyway?

Christy looked down at her lines and sighed. It was going to be hard to concentrate, with all the chaos here. She'd have to do most of her practicing at Aunt Cora's, even if it meant staying up late into the night.

She turned to another scene and scanned the page. Nearby, Marylou's brother, Vernon, began hammering on a set.

Christy sighed again. It wasn't going to be hard to concentrate, she realized. It was going to be impossible.

———

"Nice job, Christy!" Aunt Cora said that afternoon. "Very nice job!"

They'd practiced the same scene twice now, and both times, Christy had made a mess of her lines. Still, she'd gotten through the scene without thoroughly embarrassing herself, and that was something, at least.

"You're doing great," Gilroy whispered. "You're going to be the finest Juliet this theater's ever seen!"

"Thanks, Gilroy," Christy said. "Even if it's not true, it's nice to hear."

"You've got the bluest eyes I've ever seen," Gilroy said. "Except maybe for Marylou Marsh. I suppose you've got yourself lots of gentleman callers back home, huh?"

"Dozens and dozens," Christy said, but she realized from his expression that Gilroy thought she was serious. Before she could explain, Aunt Cora interrupted.

"Let's move on," she called from her front-row seat. "I want to get the staging squared away for act four, scene three, in Juliet's chamber. Christy, I want you to enter stage right. Don't worry about your lines right now. We just want to get the basic movements down. Move slowly across the stage until you reach the white bench, where you'll take your seat. Eventually, we'll have a bed there, too, but that's still being built. Got it?"

"That's simple enough that even I can handle it," Christy joked.

Christy made her way across the stage to the bench. She took her seat, trying her best to be graceful. In her head, she was reciting her lines, one by one. To her surprise, she remembered most of them.

"Fine," Aunt Cora said. "Now, after Lady Capulet enters and delivers her lines, I want you to stand and come three or four paces downstage."

Christy stood. Again, she silently recited her lines as she walked toward the edge of the stage.

Several people snickered. Christy hesitated. "Did I do something wrong?"

Gilroy pointed to her skirt. "It's your skirt, Christy. I guess the paint on that bench was still wet!"

Christy glanced over her shoulder. Sure enough, her favorite blue skirt was covered with paint.

"That bench was painted two weeks ago!" Aunt Cora cried. "How could it still be wet?"

"Someone must have put a second coat on," Arabella suggested. She strode over to Christy's side. "We professionals know to check for such things," she said. "Come on. I'll see if I can find something you can change into."

"Sorry about that, dear. Welcome to the theater," Aunt Cora said with a laugh. "I told you it's full of surprises!"

❧ Twelve ❧

"How was your first day of rehearsal?" Doctor MacNeill asked that evening at dinner.

"Humbling," Christy replied.

"She was magnificent. A natural," Aunt Cora said as she passed Christy a loaf of warm bread. "I was very proud of her."

"Aunt Cora's just being nice. I couldn't remember half my lines. I stumbled over the other half. And to top it all off, I sat on a bench covered with wet paint and ruined my skirt."

"I feel so terrible about that," Aunt Cora said. "It's the strangest thing. That paint should have been dry as a bone. But as I told you, these things happen. Before you leave Knoxville, I'll take you shopping and we'll buy you a new skirt."

"Don't be silly, Aunt Cora. It doesn't matter.

I'm just sorry I'm not doing a better job for you."

"You're not quitting already, are you?" Doctor MacNeill shook his fork at Christy. "Because if you quit, then I'm definitely quitting my art lessons."

"Didn't you enjoy yourself today, Neil?" Aunt Cora asked.

"Let's just say if I were as bad a doctor as I am a painter, I wouldn't have a patient left alive."

Christy laughed. "Neil, it's only your first day. Give it time."

"I was going to say the same thing to you."

"All right, then," Christy agreed. "Another day or two. Now, if you two will excuse me, I've got some lines to go memorize."

"I'm always available to fill in as Romeo," the doctor offered.

Christy grinned. "I'll keep that in mind."

━━ ━━ ━━

The next morning at rehearsal, Christy waited in the large dressing room backstage while Aunt Cora rehearsed with some of the other actors. Christy was so busy working on her lines that she barely noticed the small figure reflected in the mirror.

"Oliver?" she asked, spinning around.

"I'm sorry to disturb you," he muttered. "I

left my hat in here the other day, when I departed in such a huff."

"I thought you were wearing one at the party."

"A different hat," he snapped. He poked around in a pile of costumes. "No matter. It's not as if anyone cares whether my head is warm. I'm sure they'd all be thrilled if I caught cold and expired."

"Oliver, don't say that. I can tell the cast is very fond of you. I think the pressure was just getting to everyone."

"*Fond!* Phooey! They hate me, all of them. And of course they *love* Cora. Sure, Cora is the perfect director. All I heard while she was away was, 'Why can't you be more like Cora, Oliver?' Well, I'm not Cora! I'm Oliver! Oliver Flump!"

"Of course you are."

He sighed. The anger seemed to vanish. "But you like her, too, no doubt. Sweet, patient Cora."

"I do. I think she's a wonderful director. But I'm sure you would be, too—in your own way."

"She'll get her comeuppance, soon enough."

"What do you mean?" Christy asked, frowning.

"I mean this play will fall apart at the seams, and *then* we'll see who the true director is!"

"Because of me, you mean? You mean the play will fall apart because I'm taking the role of Juliet?"

Oliver patted her gently on the shoulder. "It's not your fault, my dear. It's Cora's. If she had left me in charge, things would be different. I could have gotten the actors under control. Discipline, that's what they need—a firm hand."

"I hope I don't ruin everything," Christy said forlornly.

"You won't ruin the play, Christy. Fate will. And when that happens, everyone will recognize my true genius." Oliver buttoned his topcoat. "Well, I must be off. I'm not wanted here."

Christy watched him go. She couldn't help feeling a little resentful. She was having a hard enough time keeping her confidence up. Oliver wasn't helping matters with his gloomy predictions.

"Christy!" Arabella poked her head in the door. Her strong perfume filled the room. "Cora's calling for you."

"Here I come," Christy said, but as she stood up, a horrible ripping sound met her ears.

Arabella clucked her tongue. "I *knew* that skirt was a little tight on you."

"But . . ." Christy took another step, and her skirt ripped some more. A large patch of fabric was stuck to the chair.

"It's glued!" Christy cried. "Somebody glued my chair!"

"Don't be absurd," Arabella sniffed. "Why would anybody . . ." She examined the chair. "Sure enough." She tapped a finger on her chin. "Goodness, this *is* unfortunate. I'm not sure I've got another spare skirt."

"Well, I can't go out on stage with my petticoat showing," Christy said frantically.

"Let me see what I can rustle up. You stay put."

A few minutes later, Arabella returned. She was carrying something shiny and stiff. It looked like a pair of men's trousers, made of metal.

"What on earth is that?" Christy asked.

"Armor. From our last play, *Joan of Arc*. I think it'll fit you nicely."

"I can't wear that, Arabella!"

"Well, it's not the whole suit of armor, just the bottom. Think of it as a very well-starched pair of pants."

Christy crossed her arms over her chest. "This is ridiculous. There must be something else I can—"

"Christy!" Marylou appeared at the door. "You'd better hurry! Everybody's waitin'!"

"When there's a crisis in the theater, we all do our part," Arabella told Christy. "You must try to be cooperative."

"Oh, all right. I'll wear it. But I'm going to look completely ridiculous."

"I'm sure you'll look rather . . . charming," Arabella said.

Moments later, Christy clunked her way onto the stage. Her armor-covered legs were so stiff she could barely move. She was greeted with gales of laughter.

"Interesting fashion choice," said Aunt Cora, grinning. "But I don't think it's quite Juliet's style."

"My dress ripped," Christy said sullenly. She didn't think there was any point in explaining *how* it had ripped. If a practical joker had deliberately put glue on her chair, she didn't want to give that person the satisfaction of seeing her upset.

"Well, let's proceed. We've got a lot to cover today. Let's start with the scene in Capulet's orchard."

Aunt Cora pointed to a group of wooden trees in the center of the stage. They were five tall pieces of wood, cut and painted to resemble apple trees. A wooden stand at the base kept each tree erect.

"Juliet—I mean, Christy—you'll enter first from stage left, followed by the nurse."

Christy did as she was told. *Clank. Clank. Clank.* Every step made a horrible noise, but Christy was determined to struggle on. Behind her, she could hear the whispers and giggles of her fellow cast members.

"Fine. Stop there," Aunt Cora directed. "Now, let's hear your lines. Try to direct your voice even farther than yesterday. This is an awfully big theater, so you need to project."

Christy cleared her throat. "Gallop apace, you fiery-footed steeds—" she began.

"Even louder, dear," Aunt Cora called.

"Gallop apace, you fiery-footed—"

"Look out!" someone yelled.

Suddenly, as if in slow motion, the apple tree behind Christy began to fall. Christy lurched sideways, out of its path. The movement was too sudden for her metal-clad legs.

There was no way to regain her balance. With a horrible thud, Christy landed on her backside, as the apple tree toppled to the floor, only inches away.

"Christy! Are you all right?" Gilroy ran to her side.

"I'm fine. Although this is my worst nightmare come true," Christy admitted with a shaky laugh.

"It'd be worse with a full house," Gilroy pointed out.

"I want somebody to explain to me what just happened," Aunt Cora said sternly.

One of the stagehands examined the tree. "There's a rope attached to the bottom of this prop tree. Somebody must have yanked on it. I'm awful sorry, Christy."

"Don't worry about it," Christy said. "I'm fine. However, it may take the entire cast to help me stand up in this armor."

"I feel terrible about this," Aunt Cora said. "Here you are, doing your best to help us out, and somebody's pulling these silly pranks."

"I'll say one thing. I'm starting to get the feeling somebody doesn't want me to star in this play," Christy said with a grim smile.

❧ Thirteen ❧

I wish I could get to the bottom of this, Christy," Aunt Cora apologized, "but I still haven't got a clue about who's sabotaging this play."

Four days had passed. Christy had endured several more pranks, each one more embarrassing than the last.

"What we need is a motive," said Doctor MacNeill.

He had set up an easel in Aunt Cora's parlor and was painting his first picture. Aunt Cora and Christy were seated on the far side of the room. Nobody was allowed to see the doctor's work—at least, not yet.

"Well, since most of the pranks have been directed at me, my first choice would be Arabella," Christy said. "You have to admit, she seems awfully jealous about my getting the part of Juliet."

"In all honesty, Christy," Aunt Cora said, "I wouldn't be surprised if several of the other cast members are a little jealous of you. Not that they're being fair, but acting can be very competitive."

"Still, Arabella always seems to be around when something goes wrong."

"Of course, you could say that about any of the cast," Aunt Cora observed. "They've all been present."

"Even Oliver," Christy said. "I've seen him lurking about every single day—although he keeps a low profile."

"I knew he wouldn't be able to keep away. He lives and breathes the theater."

The doctor stepped back to examine his work, his paintbrush in midair. "Perhaps you should consider Oliver a suspect. He has a motive, too."

"He does seem very upset about not getting to direct," Christy said. "He was even predicting all kinds of bad things were going to happen."

Aunt Cora just laughed. "Oh, that's just Oliver. He predicts dire things every day of his life. It's just his way. He's a born pessimist."

"Well, all I know is, I've suffered through wet paint, a falling tree, glue-ruined clothes, chairs collapsing when I went to sit in them, and a large beetle magically appearing in my ham sandwich."

"In all fairness, that may have been the beetle's idea," Doctor MacNeill said.

"Watch what you say, Neil," Christy warned, "or I'll come over there and look at your painting!"

"My masterpiece?" the doctor cried. "No one can see this until it's ready. And if I have my way, it'll *never* be ready!"

"I don't know what else to do, Christy," said Aunt Cora, wringing her hands. "I've spoken to everyone individually. I've scolded the whole group. This isn't the first time they've pulled practical jokes on new cast members, but it's definitely the worst. I just feel so awful."

"Don't. It's not your fault."

Aunt Cora checked the clock on the mantel. "Listen, I need to run a quick errand. You two sit tight. I'll be right back."

"Would you like some company?" Christy asked.

"No, no. You stay put. You've been working so hard." Aunt Cora smiled at the doctor. "We're having a surprise for dinner, by the way."

"Maybe I could help—" Christy began.

"I won't hear of it. Besides, this is my secret recipe. I think it will add a little down-home flavor you'll like."

"Sounds interesting," Christy said.

"Oh, I think it will definitely be interesting."

Christy walked Aunt Cora to the door, then returned to the parlor. "Neil, I didn't want to say anything in front of Aunt Cora, but I'm starting to wonder if maybe I should pull out of the play."

"Pull out! But you can't!" Doctor MacNeill tossed aside his paintbrush and joined Christy on the sofa. "You've been doing so well, Christy. You said so yourself. Just yesterday you were talking about how much more confident you felt on stage."

"Acting, yes. But how can I really relax when I keep waiting for the next practical joke? Somebody wants me out of that play, Neil. That's all there is to it."

"You know, at least some of those pranks affected other people. When that rolled-up curtain fell onto the stage yesterday, you and Gilroy were both there. And several people were near you when that other set toppled."

"I know. But I think that's just coincidence. I do seem to be the main target."

Christy walked over to the wall where Aunt Cora had her theater posters displayed. "I keep thinking about what Miss Alice told me. About how I should ask myself what the worst thing that could happen would be. I *thought* it would be falling on the stage in front of people. Well, I've done that, and then some."

"But you're still worried?"

Christy touched one of the framed posters and sighed. "I'm afraid something even worse may happen opening night. I might even get hurt. Lots of people might."

"Maybe you're right to be worried," the doctor said, joining her. He gave her a gentle hug. "I've been making light of all this because Aunt Cora said the actors often initiate new cast members with practical jokes. But if you're afraid, I think you should pull out. They can always do the play next year."

"I'd hate to disappoint everyone. Especially Aunt Cora. But I'm starting to feel like it's my only choice."

"Maybe if you give it another day—"

"Neil, the show's in two days. I need to make a decision soon." Christy started for the dining room. "In the meantime, if Aunt Cora's making us a special dinner, the least I can do is set the table."

"Want help?"

"No. You stay and finish your master-piece."

While she set the table, Christy practiced what she would say to Aunt Cora. *I'm sorry, Aunt Cora, but I just can't take the risk of performing. Maybe some other time. Maybe some other role . . .*

But of course, there would be no other

role. This was her chance. Her one big chance.

Christy was just setting the last plate into place when she heard the front door open. "Aunt Cora?" she called, but nobody answered.

She heard loud whispers, followed by a shrill giggle.

Christy headed toward the hall. "Aunt Cora, is that you?"

"It's us, Miz Christy!" a childish voice cried.

Christy turned the corner and stared in disbelief.

There in the hall stood Aunt Cora, along with what looked like half the population of Cutter Gap.

"Ruby Mae!" Christy cried. "Creed! Little Burl! Miss Alice!" She counted eleven students, plus Miss Alice.

"Aunt Cora done paid for our tickets so we could come and see you actin'!" Creed explained.

"I made arrangements with Miss Alice before I left Cutter Gap," Aunt Cora said. "Of course, then I thought you'd only have a small walk-on role!"

"I can't believe you're all here," Christy whispered.

"I would have arranged for the whole cove to come if I could have," Aunt Cora said. "But there just plain wasn't room. So the children drew lots to see who would come."

"David felt he could spare me for a couple days," Miss Alice said, rushing to give Christy a hug. "We're all so proud of you, Christy."

"But I was going to—" Christy began. "Aunt Cora, I really don't know . . ."

"No need to thank me, dear," Aunt Cora said breezily. "It'll be all the thanks I need when I see your friends applauding in their front-row seats!"

❧ Fourteen ❧

Well, look at you, Teacher! All gussied up so fancy-like!" Ruby Mae exclaimed the following afternoon.

The dressing room was filled to overflowing with Christy's friends from Cutter Gap. They'd just returned from a tour of the theater with Aunt Cora. She'd brought them to the dressing room to see Christy in her "Juliet finery," as Ruby Mae called it.

"You look just like a fairy princess, Miz Christy," Creed pronounced. "But how come your lips are so all-fired red?"

"That's makeup, Creed," Aunt Cora explained. "All the actors wear makeup. It's easier for the people in the audience to see their faces that way."

"Christy, are you certain you don't mind having all of us in the audience for the dress rehearsal today?" Miss Alice asked.

"I might as well get used to having a real audience," Christy said gamely. *Since it looks like I'm going through with this, after all,* she added to herself. "Let's just hope nothing goes wrong today."

"I'm sure everyone will be on their best behavior," Aunt Cora said. "After all, we open tomorrow. I doubt you'll have any more trouble with your prankster."

Arabella poked her head in the door. "I see the costume fits," she said, smiling at Christy's flowing blue gown.

"I'm all set, except that I can't seem to locate those shoes I was supposed to wear," Christy said. "I've looked everywhere."

"Let me scout around," Arabella said. "You go on ahead."

While her Cutter Gap friends gathered in the audience, Christy joined her fellow actors onstage.

"Nervous?" Gilroy asked.

Christy nodded. "I seem to have swallowed a hundred butterflies."

"I get that way, too, a little," Gilroy admitted. "'Course, I'm even worse around girls I like. I get so nervous, I just start jabbering like a jaybird. Like when I'm around Marylou, for instance."

"Gilbert, do you have a crush on Marylou?"

"She isn't easy to talk to, like you are. But she does have the most beautiful smile. . . "

Gilroy shrugged. "Lately, this past week or so, she won't even give me the time of day. I guess she has her eye on some other fella."

"Where is Marylou, anyway?"

"Running around like a chicken with her head cut off." Gilbert grinned. "Ol' Ara-bellow keeps her hopping."

Just then, Oliver tapped Christy on the shoulder. It was the first time he'd made an appearance backstage, although she'd seen him several times, watching the play from one of the rear seats.

"Oliver!" she exclaimed.

"I just wanted to wish you the best," he said. "I expect you'll need it, the way things have been going. So as we say in the theater, break a leg, my dear." He chuckled to himself. "Plenty of other things have certainly been breaking around here."

Just then, Arabella appeared, carrying the black leather ballet slippers Christy was supposed to wear with her costume. "Here you go, dear," she said, placing the slippers on the floor. "By the way, you look simply lovely."

"Thanks, Arabella." Christy eased her left foot into the slipper. "It really is a beautiful cos—"

"Is something wrong?" Arabella inquired.

"There's something in my slipper! It . . . it feels sort of . . ."

Christy curled her nose. A smell—a horrible, stomach-turning stench was filling the air.

Instantly, she knew what it was—the smell of a rotten egg.

"What *is* that appalling odor?" Arabella pinched her nose. "Christy, don't be offended, but is that *you*, dear?"

Christy pulled off her shoe, revealing the gooey remains of an egg.

"I think you know what that smell is, Arabella! You're the one who brought me the slippers. It's pretty easy to figure out that you're the one who put the egg there!"

"I did no such thing!" Arabella cried indignantly. "Where would someone of my stature get a rotten egg?"

"Would somebody *please* tell me what that vile smell is?" Aunt Cora called from her seat in the front row.

"Can you smell it down there?" Gilroy asked, waving his hand in front of his face.

"They could smell that odor in California," Aunt Cora said.

"Somebody put a rotten egg in my shoe!" Christy cried. She felt hot tears forming, but willed them to stop.

Aunt Cora leapt to her feet. "This whole thing has gone quite far enough!" she yelled. "I want whoever is behind this to step forward right this instant!"

Christy glared at Arabella.

"I had nothing to do with this, I'm telling you!" Arabella said. "Why, the smell is making me positively faint!"

Christy turned to Oliver.

"I said, 'Break a leg,'" he said. "Not 'Break an egg.'"

Christy surveyed the rest of her fellow cast members. They all seemed to be looking at her with complete sympathy. But that didn't matter. One of these people was trying to hurt and embarrass her. And she'd had enough.

"That does it," Christy said. "I am nervous enough about this without having to be afraid a prop's going to fall on me. I'm tired of being humiliated this way."

"Christy," Gilroy said, "you know we're all behind you."

"Most of you are, I know. But I've made my decision, Gilroy. I am not going out on stage tomorrow night. You'll just have to cancel the play."

⊱ Fifteen ⊱

I just can't help feeling like I've let every-one down," Christy said.

It was evening, and Christy was sitting in Aunt Cora's parlor with her friends from Cutter Gap. A fire crackled in the fireplace. Outside, light rain trickled down the windowpanes.

"Nonsense, Christy." Aunt Cora squeezed her hand. "We all understand."

"But the cast and crew . . . all their hard work will go down the drain." Christy leaned back in her chair and sighed. "Yours, too, Aunt Cora. Plus, I'll be disappointing all these friends who came from Cutter Gap just to see me."

"Don't you fret none, Miz Christy," said Creed. "We got to ride a train and we got to stay in Aunt Cora's fancy house. And we got to step inside a real, live theater."

"Creed's right," said Ruby Mae in a comforting voice. "That's plenty of fun for us. 'Course, we *was* a-hopin' to see you actin' up a storm as Juliet."

"I was, too, Ruby Mae," said Christy. "But you all understand, don't you? How could I go out on that stage tomorrow night, knowing something awful could go wrong? It was bad enough when I was just afraid I'd forget my lines or fall down. Now I have to be afraid it will start raining rotten eggs during the balcony scene. And what if someone got hurt?"

"That sure would be a sight to behold!" said Little Burl.

Christy managed a smile. "Back at the theater I felt certain I'd made the right decision. But now, I feel lousy about it. So many people were counting on me."

"You know, the theater is a little like life, isn't it?" Miss Alice reflected.

"Like Shakespeare said: 'All the world's a stage,'" Aunt Cora quoted.

"It seems to me that in our lives we can't always predict what will happen," Miss Alice said. "People get sick. Or they lose their jobs. Or bad weather strikes . . ."

"We've certainly seen our share of those things in Cutter Gap," said Doctor MacNeill. "We've had typhoid, poverty, and floods."

"But the way we get from one day to the next is to have faith that if we trust in God to help us, we can triumph over any adversity," Miss Alice said. She smiled. "Even over a storm of rotten eggs."

Christy looked at the hopeful, innocent faces of her students. She knew what Miss Alice was saying. She meant that this was Christy's chance to teach the children something far more valuable than any grammar or spelling lesson.

"Aunt Cora," Christy said firmly, "call the cast. I'm going to go through with this play, after all. Eggs or no eggs."

"Miz Christy!" Little Burl cried. "You're a-goin' to be Juliet, after all?"

"I'm going to try, Little Burl."

Aunt Cora hugged her close. "You won't regret this, I promise. I'll have the cast keep such a close watch on you, there won't be a chance for anyone to pull another prank."

"I'll be fine, no matter what," Christy said. "Miss Alice is right. I just have to have faith."

"Are you for sure and certain, Miz Christy?" Ruby Mae asked doubtfully.

"For sure and certain. I promise I won't change my mind again. I can't let one person ruin the play for everyone else."

"Was that the front door?" Aunt Cora asked.

"I'll get it," Ruby Mae volunteered.

A moment later, she returned with Marylou. "Hello, everybody," Marylou said softly.

"Marylou! What brings you here?" said Doctor MacNeill.

"Hello, Neil." Marylou smiled shyly. "I just came to bring Christy her coat." She handed it to Christy. "I guess you left it in the dressing room today."

"I was in a bit of a hurry," Christy said. "Thanks, Marylou."

"What a sweet girl, to come out in this rain!" Miss Alice exclaimed.

"I didn't mind. I wanted to come and say a proper goodbye to Christy and Neil . . ." Marylou cast a quick glance in his direction. "I guess you'll be leavin' now, what with the play canceled and all. I just want you to know I feel right bad about the way things turned out."

"Actually, there's been a change in plans. I've decided to go through with the play, after all."

"You have?" Marylou asked, clearly surprised. She hesitated. "Well, that's really good news, Christy. Yes, it is."

"Marylou, maybe you could help me get in touch with the cast and crew," Aunt Cora said.

"Sure. I'd be happy to."

Aunt Cora smiled gratefully. "You've been such a great help during this play, Marylou."

"Thank you."

"I left the cast list in the kitchen. I'll get it and we can divide up the names between us," Aunt Cora said.

"Bye, Neil. I guess you'll be there tomorrow?" Marylou asked.

"I wouldn't miss it for the world." He patted Christy's shoulder. "I intend to have a front-row seat for Christy's debut."

"You might want to reconsider where you sit. There's always the danger you'll be pelted by rotten eggs," Christy warned.

"I'll take my chances," the doctor said.

＊ ＊ ＊

"Miz Christy? Would you help me brush these snarls outa my hair?" Ruby Mae asked that evening. "It's so tangled up I'm afeared I'll pull my whole head off if'n I tug any harder."

"Sure." Carefully, Christy began to brush through Ruby Mae's wild, red hair.

"I'm awful glad you decided to be Juliet," Ruby Mae said, wincing slightly.

"Me too—I think."

"When I grow up, I might just be an actress, too."

"You'd be good at it," Christy said with an affectionate smile. "You certainly know how to act like you've done your homework when you really haven't."

Ruby Mae ignored the remark. "That gal

who came with your coat today. What part does she play?"

"Marylou? She works behind the scenes, helping the director and the costume designer." Christy tugged on a particularly tough tangle. "Sorry. I have to pull a little. You know, Marylou and the doctor were friends when they were younger."

"Sweethearts?"

"I doubt it," Christy replied. "She used to beat him up every chance she got!"

Ruby Mae laughed. "Oh, they was sweethearts for sure, then."

"Why do you say that?"

"Well, when *I* was a little 'un, I used to beat up on boys regular as could be when I was sweet on 'em."

Christy stopped brushing. "You mean it was a sign of affection?"

"Oh, yes'm. Nothin' serious, mind you. No broken bones or nothin'. Just wrasslin'."

"Really?"

"Sure. If I didn't like 'em, why would I have bothered to take the time to whop 'em so good?"

Christy considered for a moment. "Ruby Mae," she said, nodding, "I believe you've just provided me with a very interesting clue."

❧ Sixteen ❧

Two and a half hours till show time," Aunt Cora said to Christy the following evening. "How are you holding up?"

"I'm a nervous wreck," Christy admitted. She was sitting patiently in the dressing room while Arabella applied Christy's stage makeup.

"Try not to move your mouth," Arabella grumbled.

"Don't worry, Christy. You're supposed to be a nervous wreck," Aunt Cora said. "It goes with the territory." She headed for the door. "I've got to go make sure the programs are here. Anything you need?"

"Just a dose of courage."

"Nonsense, you've got plenty to spare."

Arabella stood back, staring at Christy critically. "A little more rouge, I think," she murmured. "You may need a touch-up later, by the way. I don't know why you insisted on getting ready so early. You're practically the first cast member here tonight."

"I have something I need to do before the show starts," Christy replied.

"Well, just don't muss up my fine handiwork." Arabella dabbed some pink color on Christy's cheeks. "There. The perfect Juliet. Thanks, in no small part, to me."

"Arabella," Christy said softly, "I want to apologize for accusing you about the rotten egg. It was wrong of me, and I'm sorry."

"Apology accepted. We all get a bit cranky sometimes. And I know you're under a lot of pressure." She tucked a wisp of hair behind Christy's ear. "But don't worry, darling. You're going to knock 'em dead."

"Thanks, Arabella."

When Arabella left, Christy stared at her reflection in the big mirror on the wall. "O Romeo, Romeo, wherefore art thou Romeo?" she whispered.

Her voice was trembling. So were her hands. Two and half hours till the curtain rose, and already she was so nervous she could barely whisper her lines. How would she ever make it through the night?

With a sigh, Christy climbed out of her chair. There was no point in feeling sorry for herself. She had work to do. She was going to try to keep this play from being sabotaged. And she didn't have much time.

— — —

Fifteen minutes had passed. The backstage area was still practically deserted. After this afternoon's final rehearsal, most of the cast had headed home to rest before the show.

But if someone was planning on sabotaging the play, Christy reasoned, they'd probably show up early to set things up. Why would they risk getting caught closer to show time? By then, everybody would be on the lookout for the person who'd been causing all the trouble.

Christy leaned against a wall and sighed. Maybe she should give up. There was no sign of Marylou—or of anyone else, for that matter.

Just as she turned down a hallway, Christy noticed Marylou's younger brother, Vernon, stepping into the storage area where the costumes were kept. He closed the door behind him.

Christy tiptoed down the hall and put her ear to the door. Carefully, she turned the door handle and opened the door a crack.

Vernon's back was to the door. He was in the far corner of the dimly-lit room. A lamplight flickered. Huge shadows danced on the wall.

Christy watched in shock as he pulled her costume off a rack and turned the gown inside-out.

Gently, slowly, Christy eased into the room and slipped behind a rack of costumes.

Vernon didn't seem to notice. He pulled a metal can out of his pocket and opened the top. Then he upended the can and began shaking it over Christy's costume. Out rained a fine powder.

Suddenly, the door flew open.

"Vernon!" Marylou cried. "What are you doing? I told you no more, and I meant it!"

"B—but Marylou! What's the point, if we don't do something tonight, of all nights? I thought you *wanted* me to do this."

"Not anymore." Marylou sighed. "After I went over to Cora's yesterday, I could see the way Neil was lookin' at Christy. I realized he's never goin' to look at me that way, Vernon. Most likely, no fella ever will."

Christy stepped out from behind the rack of clothes.

"Sakes alive!" Vernon cried, leaping backward. The can of powder dropped to the floor.

"You've been behind this whole thing, haven't you, Marylou?" Christy asked, trying to rein in her fury.

Marylou's shoulders slumped. "Yes. And I'm awful sorry, Christy, not that sayin' so does much good now. I was just . . . hurtin', I suppose."

"You mean because you've always had a crush on Neil?"

"For as long as I can remember. And then, when he came back to Knoxville, saying how we ought to get together and all, and then nothing came of it. . . . Besides, I could see you were sweet on each other." She wiped away a tear. "I've got no excuse, Christy."

"So you recruited Vernon to help you set up your tricks?"

Vernon grinned proudly. "I came up with this one all on my own!"

"What's in the can, Vernon?" Christy asked.

"Itchin' powder."

Marylou groaned. "I *told* him no more. I started thinkin' on how sad everyone was goin' to be, if the play was canceled. Even ol' Ara-bellow."

"I couldn't help myself," Vernon said with a giggle. "It was such a fine trick, don't you see?"

Christy managed a smile. "Yes, it certainly was ingenious, Vernon. Only now what am I going to do?"

"Maybe we could wash off the powder," Marylou suggested.

"Nope." Vernon shook his head. "It sticks like glue. That was my doin', too, by the way," he added proudly. "Remember the glue on the chair?"

"You're quite the mischief-maker, Vernon," Christy said. "I've got a couple of students just like you."

Marylou thumbed through the racks of clothes. "I've got it!" she said. "Although it may take a little work." She pulled out a long, pale green dress.

"It looks like my gown," Christy said. "But it's about three sizes too big."

"Not by the time I'm done with it. We've got two hours. And nobody stitches faster than I do."

"Do you really think you can do it?"

"You just wait, Christy. I'll have this dress ready for you before you know it!" Marylou paused. "But there's just one condition."

"Yes?"

"You promise to forgive me for the rotten way I've been actin'."

Christy gave her a hug. "Of course I forgive you. By the way, you're wrong about one thing."

"What's that?"

"You said no fellow would ever look at you the way Neil looks at me. But I know that a member of the cast has a secret crush on you."

"You're just pullin' my leg."

"Nope," Christy smiled. "It just so happens he goes by the name of Romeo."

❧ Seventeen ❧

There's a full house," Christy whispered, peeking out from behind the heavy, velvet curtain.

"I still don't understand why you changed your costume at the last minute like this," Arabella muttered. "It's very unprofessional. Besides, pale green will completely clash with my set."

"It'll match my complexion perfectly," Christy joked.

Aunt Cora signaled Christy. "Get ready for your entrance, Juliet," she whispered.

Christy took a deep breath. She closed her eyes.

She knew the play as if she'd written it herself. She knew the set as if she'd been born there. She knew her character as if she really *were* Juliet.

It was time.

Christy stepped onto the stage.

Her throat tightened. Her heart raced.

What was her first line? She couldn't remember her line!

See? a voice inside of her taunted. *You're not ready for this, Christy. You're going to fail. You're doomed.*

Christy gazed out into the audience at the vast sea of faces.

She could feel her fellow actors waiting, holding their breath, crossing their fingers.

With God's help, I know I can do this, Christy told herself.

She closed her eyes and silently prayed. When Christy opened her eyes, she glanced down at the front row. Miss Alice was there, and so were Christy's students.

But for now, they weren't her students.

For now, the audience wasn't there.

For a few moments, while the magic of the theater lasted, her name would be Juliet, and the stage would be hers.

—— —— ——

"A stunning performance," Doctor MacNeill told Christy that evening at the cast party.

"Maybe not stunning," Christy said, "but it sure was fun! Once I started acting, I actually had a good time."

"Miz Christy," Creed tugged on Christy's arm, "could I have your writin' name?"

"My writin' name?"

"He means your autograph," Ruby Mae explained, nudging Creed out of the way. "First, sign my program, Miz Christy."

"No, mine!" Creed yelped.

"Write on mine, Teacher!" Bessie demanded.

"Suddenly, I don't feel like a star anymore." Christy winked at the doctor. "I feel like a teacher."

"You ain't a-goin' to run off and be an actor for good, are you?" Creed asked nervously.

"No, Creed. Acting's fun. But teaching's my real love."

Just as Christy had finished signing the programs, Oliver came over. "A class act!" he cried. "I knew you were a class act the minute I laid eyes on you!" He bowed and kissed her hand.

"Why, Oliver!" Christy said.

"You didn't have to invite me on stage for that last curtain call," Oliver said. "Not after the way I've been acting. But it was a real honor to share the stage with such a pro. Now, if you'll excuse me, I've got business to discuss with Cora. I'm hoping she'll let me direct our *next* play . . ."

"That was awfully thoughtful of you," the doctor said.

"He's a sweet man," Christy said, "even if

he *can* be a little difficult." She pulled the doctor aside. "By the way, you and I had a deal. Fair is fair. It's time for you to unveil your painting."

The doctor groaned. "I was hoping you'd forget."

"Not on your life."

"Come on, then. It's over in the corner, covered by a sheet. Just don't let anybody else see it."

Before he removed the covering, Doctor MacNeill held up a warning finger. "Don't forget this is my first effort."

"I understand. Let me guess—I'll bet it's a painting of the mountains. The view from your cabin porch."

"Not exactly. Although my goal *was* to capture the beauty of the place." Suddenly, he dropped the sheet. "I can't. It's too awful. It doesn't even begin to do my subject justice."

"Neil—" Christy grabbed the sheet, "let me see—"

She pulled back the sheet and gasped. A smile came to her lips. "It's . . . it's . . . me!"

"Not even close to you," the doctor said. To Christy's surprise, he was blushing. "I mean, the nose is all wrong. And the mouth. And look at your ears! They look like elephant ears! You have wonderful ears, and I made you look like a circus animal!"

"Neil." Christy placed a gentle kiss on his

cheek. "It's wonderful. It's the most beautiful painting I've ever seen, because it came from the artist's heart. May I keep it?"

"You really want it?"

"I'd be honored to have it."

"But the ears—"

"Never mind the ears."

"All right, then," the doctor said. "But next time I paint your portrait, I'm getting the ears right."

"It's rather a mysterious smile," Christy observed.

The doctor nodded. "That's because I still haven't unlocked the secrets of your heart. Of course, if you'd let me have a peek at that diary of yours . . ."

"Don't count on it," Christy said.

━ ━ ━

That night, after everyone else was fast asleep, Christy got out her diary and pen.

She didn't want the magic of the evening to be lost, not ever. Somehow, she felt if she wrote down the right words, she'd be able to preserve the thrill forever:

It's very late, and I know I should be asleep. But it's as if the excitement of tonight is still with me—the applause, the bows, the bouquet of roses from the cast.

But the strange thing is, while it was wonderful to live out my fantasy of appearing on stage, that isn't what I'll take away with me from this night.

What matters most to me is that I faced my fear and rose above it. I had faith that with God's help I could get through a difficult time. And I was right.

But now, looking back, I can see that it was just a small fear. The important thing is that I can apply what I've learned to other challenges—harder tasks and bigger fears. As long as I remember to try my hardest and trust in God, there's no telling what I may accomplish!

✺ Eighteen ✺

"Sorry, folks. It's time for your spelling test," Christy announced, "whether you're ready or not."

A week had passed. Christy was back in Cutter Gap. Everything had returned to normal. Under David's watchful eye, the children had kept up with their lessons. After a couple of days of excitement following Christy's return, everyone had settled down.

Even for Christy, the adventure in Knoxville now seemed like a dream. It was hard to believe she'd actually set foot on that big stage—let alone that she'd taken repeated bows to thunderous applause.

"Take out your blackboards, children," Christy said. "I'm sure if you studied, you won't have any trouble with these words."

"Miz Christy?" Creed frantically waved his hand. "I got an idea."

Christy put her hands on her hips. "You've stalled as long as you can, Creed. It's time to face the music."

"How about if we do some rememberin' about goin' to Knoxville first?" Creed pleaded.

"We've done that. Repeatedly. You got to show everyone your program. We talked about what it was like to ride on a train. Bessie showed us her drawing of Aunt Cora's house. And Ruby Mae did a fine impression of me on the stage as Juliet. Don't you think we've relived Knoxville enough for one week?"

Creed sighed. "I s'pose so," he said, his face downcast. "But I just wanted to tell everybody about one more thing."

Christy had seen Creed pull this trick a dozen times—always right before a big test. But he'd looked so disappointed, she decided to relent this time.

"All right. One more thing."

Creed stood up so that everyone could hear him. "I just wanted to tell about what it was like the night of the big play."

The class fell into rapt attention. Although there had been a little jealousy from the children who hadn't been lucky enough to go to Knoxville, they never seemed to tire of hearing stories about what it had been like. Perhaps, Christy reflected, because they hoped someday they, too, would get the chance for an adventure of their own.

"The thing of it is," Creed continued, "when Miz Christy walked out onto that stage for the first time, she looked just like a fairy princess in one of those stories she's always a-tellin' us. But the best part was, she was *my* teacher, my very own! I knowed she was afeared about goin' out there, what with all the pranks and such. And there she was, sure as shootin', only she wasn't just Teacher anymore."

Ruby Mae nodded. "Nope," she said softly, "she was Juliet!"

"I tell you," Creed said, "I thought my chest was goin' to split right open, with all the pride I was feelin'!"

Listening to Creed, Christy knew with all her heart that *this* was the real stage where she belonged. This was a much tougher audience, to be sure. But their applause was what really mattered.

"Thank you, Creed," she said. "That was very sweet. But you know when I feel the most pride? When I look out at all of you and realize I'm helping you learn and grow."

Creed raised his hand again. "Miz Christy? I got another bit of tellin' to do—"

Christy laughed. "Nice try, Creed. But you can't stall forever. Maybe later, we can do some more telling. Right now, it's time for some *spelling*."

Her announcement was met with loud groans. But to Christy, it was a sweeter sound than all the applause in the world.

Goodbye,
Sweet Prince

The Characters

CHRISTY RUDD HUDDLESTON, a nineteen-year-old girl.

CHRISTY'S STUDENTS:
    CREED ALLEN, age nine.
    LITTLE BURL ALLEN, age six.
    DELLA MAY ALLEN, age eight.
    ROB ALLEN, age fourteen.
    WANDA BECK, age eight.
    BESSIE COBURN, age twelve.
    WRAIGHT HOLT, age seventeen.
    RUBY MAE MORRISON, age thirteen.
    MOUNTIE O'TEALE, age ten.
    CLARA SPENCER, age twelve.
    LUNDY TAYLOR, age seventeen.
    HANNAH WASHINGTON, age eight.

DAVID GRANTLAND, the young minister.
IDA GRANTLAND, David's sister, and mission housekeeper.

ALICE HENDERSON, a Quaker missionary who started the mission at Cutter Gap.

DR. NEIL MACNEILL, the physician of the Cove.

BEN PENTLAND, the mailman for the Cove.

BIRD'S-EYE TAYLOR, the father of Christy's student Lundy.

MRS. TATUM, a woman who runs a boarding house in El Pano.

JARED COLLINS, the owner of Great Oak Farm.

URIAH WYNNE, an employee on Great Oak Farm.

HANK DREW, the mailman for the area that includes Great Oak Farm.

KETTIE WELLER, a mother of twins.

SHERIFF BELL, the local sheriff.

PRINCE, a black stallion.

OLD THEO, a mule owned by the mission.

GOLDIE, Miss Alice's mare.

✤ One ✤

Happy birthday!"

"Look how big he's grown!"

"I can't wait for him to open his presents!"

Christy Huddleston's students crowded around the birthday boy, applauding and singing.

He stared at them, blinked, then let out a loud snort.

Christy laughed. For a horse, it was a perfectly polite response. "I think Prince wonders what the fuss is all about," she said.

Christy was sitting on the rail fence that enclosed the black stallion's pasture. Her entire class—all seventy students—had gathered there to celebrate Prince's birthday.

The class was supposed to be studying geography this afternoon. But Christy had decided that the children deserved this special treat. Lately, Cutter Gap had fallen on particularly hard times. It was nice to have a reason to celebrate *something*—even if it was just the birthday of a horse.

Of course, Prince wasn't just *any* horse. The magnificent stallion had somehow managed to cast a magic spell over her students. The shy ones grew braver around Prince. The clumsy ones grew confident as they trotted around the pasture on his broad back. And the troublemakers actually seemed to grow calmer. Even Lundy Taylor, the worst bully in the school, acted like a different person around Prince.

Ruby Mae Morrison stepped forward and cleared her throat. "It's time for the present-givin'," she announced.

Quickly, the children fell silent. They'd been planning this for weeks. Ruby Mae, who was thirteen, had been chosen to present Prince's gifts. Although he belonged to the mission, it was Ruby Mae, more than anyone else, who cared for Prince. With the help of the mission minister, David Grantland, she fed Prince, groomed him, and exercised him every day. She was also the most accomplished rider of all the children.

"Before we start," Ruby Mae announced, "I have to tell the truth. We don't rightly know for sure and certain that today is Prince's birthday." Gently, she scratched the stallion's nose. "Since he was a present to the mission, nobody exactly knows when he was born, 'ceptin' that he's about three years old. But I took a vote, and we figured today would be a fine day to have a birthday."

Bessie Coburn, one of Ruby Mae's best friends, elbowed Ruby Mae in the ribs. "The presents, Ruby Mae! Get to the presents!"

"All right, then. First off, the necklace!"

Hannah Washington and Della May Allen paraded over solemnly, carrying a large round garland. It was made of woven twigs, flowers, and berries. Carefully, they placed it around Prince's glossy neck.

"He's eatin' the berries!" Hannah exclaimed. "He likes it!"

Everyone laughed. It was a nice moment, one that Christy had feared she would never see when Hannah's family, the descendants of slaves, had first come to this isolated mountain cove. Her dark skin had set her apart, and it had broken Christy's heart to see the ignorance and prejudice Hannah and her family had endured.

But Hannah had persevered, and Prince had done his part to help her. Like Ruby Mae, Hannah was a gifted rider. By offering to teach several of the children what she knew about riding, she'd found a way to reach them and to make some real friends.

"And now," Ruby Mae continued, "for the next present!"

Mountie O'Teale stepped up to Prince's side. She was a small girl for her ten years, shy and self-conscious around strangers because of a lingering speech problem. Still, whenever Mountie was around Prince, she blossomed. Her speech flowed, and her smiles came quickly.

"This is for you, Prince," Mountie announced in a clear voice, rich with the mountain accent Christy never tired of hearing. "It's for keepin' you warm on winter nights. And we all put in a bit of it."

Mountie held out the precious gift—a horse blanket sewn together like a patchwork quilt. With Ruby Mae's help, she placed the blanket over Prince's back.

As Mountie adjusted the blanket, Christy's eyes filled with tears. A square of fabric was missing from the sleeve of Mountie's worn, tattered dress. The other children had similar missing patches, since they'd each donated a piece of fabric for the quilt.

"It's beautiful, children," Christy said softly. "Prince is a very lucky fellow."

The blanket had been the children's idea. Christy had resisted the notion at first, knowing how little they could afford to sacrifice— even a square inch of clothing. As it was, most of the children were shoeless year-round, and they all wore hand-me-downs or donations from churches. To cut into those precious clothes for a horse's birthday present? As much as Christy understood their desire to give, she just didn't think it was a sacrifice they could afford to make.

But one evening, Miss Alice Henderson, the woman who had helped found the mission, had taken Christy aside. "'It is more blessed to give than to receive,'" she'd told Christy. "Perhaps this is a sacrifice the children would like to make."

"But now?" Christy had asked. "The mission's never been so short on donations and cash. We've been scraping by for weeks, living on hope and prayers. The last thing the children need is to be giving away the clothes off their own backs. For a horse's birthday, no less!"

"Maybe," Miss Alice had replied, "that's exactly why they need it. Maybe Prince's birthday provides them with a reason to celebrate. We all need to be able to give, Christy."

Out had come the scissors. One by one, Christy had cut tiny squares out of her students' precious clothes.

"It's just like Joseph's coat o' many colors!" Ruby Mae exclaimed. "Ain't it just the purtiest thing you ever did see?"

As if on command, Prince sauntered around in a circle, showing off his new blanket and garland. With his head held high and his mane streaming in the wind, he was a wonderful sight.

"Would you look at that?" David called as he strode toward the fence. "Children, that is, without a doubt, the finest horse blanket in the history of horse blankets! And look how Prince is dancing about! I can tell he loves it. Judging from the way he's trying to eat his garland, he seems to love that, too!"

Prince trotted around while the children followed him, laughing and joking. "I haven't seen them in such a good mood in a long time," Christy whispered to David. "It's good to see. They love that horse so much."

A frown creased David's brow. He glanced back at the mission house.

"David?" Christy asked. "What's wrong?"

"I . . ." He paused. "The truth is, Christy, I'm not sure how much longer we're going to be able to keep Prince."

༺ TWO ༺

"Miss Ida," Christy said at dinner that evening, "that was a very nice soup. What do you call it?"

"Whatever Soup," said Miss Ida, who was David's sister. "I toss whatever I can find into the pot and let it boil. Tonight it was potatoes, some roots Ruby Mae dug up, and half an onion."

"Well, at least we're not resorting to boiling shoe leather," David joked.

"Don't be too sure, David." Miss Ida started to clear the table. "Remember how tough that meat was last night?"

David gulped as Miss Ida headed to the kitchen. "She *was* joking, wasn't she?"

"Preacher, 'course she was *jokin'.*" Ruby Mae rolled her eyes. "Shoe leather's way too precious to waste on eatin'."

Miss Alice sighed. "The sad truth is, we are going to have to do some belt-tightening." She motioned toward the kitchen. "Ruby Mae, you go on and help Miss Ida clean up. Christy and David and I have some things to discuss."

"Uh-oh." Ruby Mae leapt out of her chair. "I hate discussions. There's always a heap o' loud voices. Leastways, that's how it always was with my ma and step-pa."

She grabbed her plate and mug, tossed her head, and dashed for the kitchen, her long, red hair flying like a flag in the breeze. Because Ruby Mae had a hard time getting along with her stepfather, she was living at the mission house for the time being. She could be a handful sometimes, but everyone was very fond of her.

Miss Alice led David and Christy to the parlor. She pointed to a wooden box. "Take a look," she said. "That's the latest round of donations."

Christy peeked inside. The half-empty box contained a few threadbare clothes and some musty books.

"We have to face facts," Miss Alice said. "The mission is very low on funds. We're short on food and supplies, and most importantly, on medicine."

Christy couldn't help feeling alarmed at her tone. Miss Alice was always calm in a crisis.

No matter what the problem was, she always seemed to have a solution. But today, she looked genuinely worried. Her gray eyes were rimmed in red, and the smile lines around her eyes looked more like deep worry lines.

"The mission's always struggling to make ends meet, Miss Alice," Christy pointed out. "Perhaps if I send some more letters, asking for donations—"

"This is far more serious than that, Christy." Miss Alice rubbed her eyes. "Doctor MacNeill and I are dreadfully short on medical supplies. Miss Ida is running out of food. I'm afraid this is going to call for some drastic actions."

Christy didn't know what to say. She walked to the window, trying to collect her thoughts. The deep green spires of the Great Smoky Mountains loomed in the distance. Once again, she was struck by the contrasts in this wondrous landscape. How could a land so rich in beauty be inhabited by people so desperately poor?

"I think," Miss Alice said softly, "that we only have one choice. We need to sell something of value. And the most valuable thing the mission owns is Prince."

David nodded gravely. He looked sadder than Christy had ever seen him. Christy knew he loved that horse as much as the children did.

"You're right, Miss Alice," he said softly. "There's an auction in El Pano next week. I'll take him myself."

"I'm so sorry, David. If I could think of another way . . ." Miss Alice's voice trailed off. "Old Theo wouldn't bring us much. As lame as he is, we'd have to pay somebody to take that poor old mule off our hands. And Goldie's a fine mare, but she's getting up there in years. If we didn't get enough for her, we'd have to sell Prince later on, too. And we can't afford to lose both horses. It's the only way we can get to the most remote parts of these mountains."

"But the children will be heartbroken," Christy protested. "There must be another way. Maybe if I went home to Asheville, I could ask for donations from churches. Or I could even get a job for a while. . . ."

"And how would that help the children?" Miss Alice asked. "They need you here, Christy. No, I'm afraid this is the only way."

Christy dropped into a chair next to David. For a while, nobody spoke.

Finally, Christy broke the silence. "Remember when Mr. Pentland delivered Prince to us at the school?" she asked with a wistful smile. "I can still hear him calling out 'Special delivery from the U-nited States Postal Service!' Who would ever have imagined the mailman was delivering a huge black stallion? The children were so thrilled I thought I'd never get them to settle down again!"

"It was a very generous donation," Miss Alice agreed. A woman who had met Christy's mother in Asheville, North Carolina, had sent Prince after learning of the mission's need for a horse. "And we've been blessed to have such a fine animal as a companion. But I'm sure David will find him a fine new home. Perhaps, if it's close enough, we could even take the children to visit sometimes."

Just then, Ruby Mae appeared in the doorway. "Visit who?"

"Ruby Mae," Christy said, "you know you shouldn't eavesdrop!"

"I weren't eavesdroppin'. Miss Ida done sent me to see if'n anybody wants some tea. She's got some herbs she's been savin'." She planted her hands on her hips. "So who would we be a-visitin'? The doctor's Aunt Cora in Knoxville, maybe? Or Miz Christy's folks back in Asheville?"

"No, Ruby Mae." Miss Alice cast a quick glance at Christy. "I'm afraid we've got some bad news, dear."

"What kind of bad news?"

"The mission needs money, Ruby Mae," Christy said gently. "Very, very badly. Now, you know how much we all love Prince, but—"

"Prince?" Ruby Mae asked. "What does

Prince have to do with it?" Suddenly, her eyes went wide. "Unless . . . unless you all are a-plannin' to sell him?"

"It's the only way," David said. "You know I love that horse as much as you do, Ruby Mae. You know I'd do anything to try to keep him if I could."

"You don't love him like I do!" Ruby Mae shouted. "Nobody does! You ain't the one who knows just where he likes to be scratched behind his right ear! You ain't the one who's kissed him goodnight ever' single evenin' since he come to Cutter Gap!" A sob racked her body. "Nobody loves him like I love him! You can't sell him! You just can't!"

"There isn't any choice, Ruby Mae," Christy said. She tried to embrace her, but Ruby Mae yanked free.

"I'll never forgive you for this," Ruby Mae sobbed. "Never, not as long as I live!"

She spun around and ran up the stairs. In the silence that followed, her awful sobs seemed to fill the whole house.

❧ Three ❧

I suppose most of you know that tomorrow the Reverend Grantland and Ruby Mae and I will be taking Prince to the auction in El Pano," Christy said the following Thursday morning at school. "Miss Alice will be teaching you tomorrow. I expect you all to be on your best behavior."

A few days had passed. By now, everybody knew about the decision to sell Prince. All week, Christy had dealt with the pleading and tears of her students.

Wraight Holt had threatened to kidnap Prince and hide him in a safe area no one could find. (Fortunately, Christy had talked him out of that scheme.) Creed Allen had offered to sell his new litter of hound dogs in exchange for Prince's safety. Everybody, it seemed, had a plan for saving Prince.

But in the end, there was nothing anyone could do. Standing before her class today, Christy realized that this was the hardest lesson she'd had to teach her students. How could she help the children accept a loss like this . . . children who had so little to lose and who'd suffered through so much?

She patted Clara Spencer on the shoulder. Like so many of the students, Clara's eyes were red, and she was sniffling softly.

"I know how hard this is," Christy said as she walked past the rows of desks and benches. "But loss is a part of life, children. With God's help, we'll make it through this sad time. Who knows what the future may bring? Maybe someday we'll read about Prince after he's become a famous racehorse. Can anybody else think of another happy ending to this story?"

After a moment, Creed raised his hand. "Maybe he'll grow up to be a daddy and have lots of little Princes runnin' around."

"That's a wonderful idea, Creed. Anybody else?"

"He could go to a farm where they grow lots and lots of sugar, 'cause he loves sugar more 'n anything," Little Burl Allen suggested. "And he could get fat and sassy like my ol' hound dog."

"That would be a very happy future for Prince," Christy agreed.

Ruby Mae glared at Christy. "Them's just fairy tales. Ain't but one good future for Prince," she said. "That's when we find a way to keep him here in Cutter Gap, where he belongs."

The answer didn't surprise Christy. Since she'd found out they'd have to sell Prince, Ruby Mae had barely spoken to Christy. Each evening at dinner, she simply stared at her plate. In school, she refused to answer questions. She'd spent every spare moment she could find with Prince.

"That's such a nice dream, Ruby Mae," Christy said gently. "But I think we have to accept the fact that Prince won't be living here anymore."

"I ain't never goin' to accept that," Ruby Mae muttered. Someone else sobbed. Another student sniffled.

Christy couldn't help sighing. She wanted to cry herself. She'd be very glad when this whole thing was over. With time, the children's pain would ease.

At least, that's what she hoped.

~ ~ ~

"You're sure you want to come?" David asked the next morning. "It's a long, hard walk to El Pano. And I'm sure you remember how tough the trail can be, Christy."

"Don't try to talk me out of it, David," Christy answered. "I'm coming."

"I'm comin', too, no matter what you say," Ruby Mae agreed. "I got to say goodbye, proper-like."

It was a cool, breezy day. Wisps of clouds flew past the mountaintops like ships on a pale blue ocean. In the pasture, Prince was grazing calmly.

"Look how happy Prince is. He don't even know what's a-comin'," Ruby Mae said. "He thinks he can trust us."

"I know you think we're betraying Prince, Ruby Mae," David said as he leaned against the fence. "But we're going to make sure he gets a good home. I promise."

Ruby Mae jutted her chin. "S'posin' *your* ma and pa sold you? How do you think that'd make you feel?"

"It's not like that, Ruby Mae," Christy said. But even as she said the words, she realized that for Ruby Mae, this goodbye was probably especially hard. Perhaps she felt a little abandoned herself, living with Christy and Miss Ida at the mission house. Ruby Mae hardly ever saw her mother or her stepfather. Watching Prince being torn from his "family" couldn't be easy. Still, she did at least seem somewhat more resigned to the fact that he was leaving.

Off in the distance came the sound of a

galloping horse. "Looks like Doctor MacNeill," Ruby Mae reported. "And there's someone ridin' with him."

"That's Lundy Taylor!" Christy exclaimed.

Doctor MacNeill reined his horse to a stop, and he and Lundy dismounted. "Thought I'd stop by to wish you a safe trip," the doctor said, winking at Christy.

David pretended to bat his eyes. "Why, Neil, I didn't know you cared!"

The doctor laughed. "Actually, I was talking to Christy, Reverend."

"Now, there's a surprise," David said. David and Neil had been rivals for Christy's affections for some time.

"In any case, it was nice of you to come, Neil," Christy said. "And what brings you here, Lundy?"

Lundy shrugged. "Doc and me crossed paths up yonder on the ridge. Said he'd give me a ride."

"Lundy has something he wants to give to Prince," the doctor explained. He pointed to the burlap sack Lundy had hoisted over his shoulder.

Lundy grimaced. He was a dark, hulking young man with a threatening swagger. Christy had always been a little bit afraid of him, although she tried not to show it. But today, strangely enough, Lundy seemed almost shy.

"Ain't nothin' much," Lundy said.

"Figures," muttered Ruby Mae. Like most of Christy's students, she wasn't exactly fond of the bully.

"Well, we'd better call Prince over here," David said. "You know how he loves gifts."

He let out a shrill whistle. Instantly, Prince swung around and trotted over to the fence. Lundy reached up and scratched the stallion's nose. "Hey, ol' Prince. Looky here. I brung you somethin'. On account o' your goin' away and all."

Ruby Mae looked a little annoyed. "We already done all the presents at his birthday party, Lundy."

"This is different," Lundy said, his eyes locked on Prince. "This is . . . special. He ain't just yours, Ruby Mae Morrison."

Lundy reached into the burlap sack and pulled out a simple, homely bridle. He held it out and Prince sniffed at it happily.

"I made it outa some deer hide I was a-savin'. Pa said I was a fool to waste it." Lundy hesitated. "Whopped me good over it, truth to tell."

Christy winced. Lundy's father, Bird's-Eye, had a notorious bad temper.

"It's beautiful, Lundy," she said.

"No, it ain't," Lundy replied matter-of-factly. "I ain't much for makin' things. But the leather's soft as it comes. It'll feel nice on his face. And see? I cut his name into the leather."

He held up the bridle. Sure enough, he'd crudely carved letters into the leather:

PRINS

Christy saw Ruby Mae open her mouth to speak. She knew what was coming next—some nasty comment about the bridle, or the fact that Lundy did so poorly in school. Goodness knew that Lundy deserved the wrath of his fellow students, as much as he'd bullied them all. Still, Christy couldn't help cringing as she waited for the hurtful remark.

"It's . . ." Ruby Mae's gaze darted from Lundy to Prince and back again. Lundy touched the stallion's nose, his eyes filled with tears.

Ruby Mae took a deep breath. "It's a wondrous bridle, Lundy," she said softly. "Prince'll be mighty proud to wear it, I reckon."

"Thanks, Ruby Mae," Lundy whispered.

Ruby Mae hopped over the fence and gestured for Lundy to follow. "Come on. I'll help you put it on him. He'll be the finest horse for sure at the auction." She shook her head. "Much as it hurts me to say so."

❧ Four ❧

It's such a shame, havin' to sell that fine animal. But I'm sure you'll get yourselves a fair price," said Mrs. Tatum, the owner of the boarding house in El Pano.

It was Saturday morning. Christy, Ruby Mae, and David had spent the night in Mrs. Tatum's Victorian frame house. It was the same place Christy had stayed when she had first come to Tennessee some months ago.

"I want to thank you again for taking us in, Mrs. Tatum," David said, "and I promise you that as soon as we sell Prince, we'll pay you for our rooms."

"Nonsense," said the tall, big-boned woman. "I wouldn't hear of it. Me, take money from a man of the cloth and a fine teacher like Miss Huddleston? Not likely." She slipped a basket over Ruby Mae's arm. "Now, there's plenty of my famous spareribs and pickled beans in here to keep you goin'."

"Mrs. Tatum, you're too kind," Christy said.

"I'm just glad to see you've survived in Cutter Gap." Mrs. Tatum smiled at David. "To tell you the truth, I didn't think this mite of a gal, all of nineteen years, would last a week in that out-of-the-way place. It's a miracle, I tell you."

"Christy's tougher than she looks, believe me," David said fondly.

"Well, I guess you'd best be gettin' on. The auction barn's about a quarter mile down yonder. You can't miss it. There'll be folks comin' from miles around. Most of them are just there to watch, not to buy. There's maybe half a dozen big spenders. And 'course, there's Mr. Jared Collins."

"Who's he?" Ruby Mae asked.

"Just the richest man in these here parts. Owns Great Oak Farm, and makes most of his money buyin' and sellin' horses. He's quite the fancy gentleman. You can't miss him. Just look for the golden riding crop. He carries it everywhere with him."

David and Christy set off toward the auction barn, with Ruby Mae astride Prince. Mrs. Tatum had been right. The barn was easy to find. A steady stream of people were heading in that direction.

"You know," Ruby Mae said, "I was just thinkin'. This'll be the last time I ride Prince, forever and ever." She cast a desperate look at David. "Preacher, you sure there ain't some other way?"

"I'm sure, Ruby Mae."

She gave a resigned nod and said nothing more until they reached the auction site.

The auction barn was bustling with activity. It smelled of hay and leather and horse. The center was ringed off, and around the ring were bleachers where observers and bidders could watch the horses come and go. Most of the people there looked like simple farmers, dressed in plain clothes or overalls. But a few, as Mrs. Tatum had predicted, looked very well-to-do.

David went to talk to one of the auctioneers. He returned a few minutes later. "We're supposed to take Prince to stall number one," he explained. "The bidders will come by to take a look at him before the actual auction takes place."

"Then what?" Ruby Mae asked.

"Then we wait for his number to be called, and they'll lead him into the center ring for the bidding. Since he's number one, he'll probably be the first horse out."

The stalls were located on the far side of the barn. Ruby Mae led Prince into the stall marked "one." Next door, a young boy was busily brushing the mane of a dapple gray mare.

When he saw Prince, he let out a low

whistle. "Whoa. He's bound to fetch a pretty penny," he said.

Ruby Mae didn't answer. The boy held out his brush. "Want to clean him up? He'll get a better bid if'n he's lookin' shiny."

"Prince don't need no brush," Ruby Mae said. "He's already plenty beautiful."

"Suit yourself."

Down the aisle came prospective buyers, one by one. All of them, it seemed, stopped to admire Prince.

The first was a tall man with small, black eyes. He was accompanied by a shorter, grizzled-looking companion.

"My name's Lyle Duster," the tall man said. "This here's my brother Ed." Ed coughed softly and stared at the ground. Lyle eyed Prince appreciatively.

"Nice piece o' horseflesh," he muttered.

"Mr. Duster, Prince ain't no horseflesh," Ruby Mae replied angrily. "He's a fine animal who just happens to be my friend."

Mr. Duster ignored her.

"An animal like that would do for all our farm work. He's plenty strong to do all the plowin' and run races on weekends, as well."

Ed nodded mutely. David cleared his throat. "I'm sorry, gentlemen, but Prince is only for sale to an owner who won't overwork him. We love him too much to let him work seven days a week."

Lyle Duster spat rudely. "I reckon there's other ways o' gettin' what we want." Ed laughed softly as they walked away.

"Them people give me the willies," Ruby Mae half-whispered to Christy. "Do you reckon they could be thinkin' of stealin' Prince?"

"I certainly hope not," Christy replied. "It sounds as if those people shouldn't own a horse."

A young couple dressed in Sunday finery stopped next. "Clean gaits?" the man asked as he knelt to examine Prince's legs.

"Oh, he's a dream to ride," David replied.

"If'n you don't mind usin' a pillow with your saddle," Ruby Mae muttered under her breath.

"Ruby Mae," Christy scolded when the couple was out of hearing, "there's no point in saying unkind things about Prince. One way or another, he's going to be sold today."

"I know. It's just I hate the way they come and go, pokin' and proddin' like he's a piece o' fruit for sale. He's a livin' creature, Miz Christy. He's got feelings."

"Well, how do you think he feels, hearing you say those things about him?"

"Oh, he don't mind. He knows I'm on his side."

A few minutes later, a tall man with slicked-back hair and a dark mustache paused in front of Prince's stall. He sported a black riding coat and a satin top hat, and in his hand was a riding crop topped with a gold handle.

"Miz Tatum told us about you," Ruby Mae said. "You're the man with all the horses."

"Jared Collins, at your service," the man said, removing his hat and bowing low.

"Are you rich?" Ruby Mae asked.

"Rich? Ah, well, that's all relative, isn't it, my dear? Blessed, perhaps. It's true I do own a few horses. None, I must say, as fine a specimen as this. May I enter the stall?"

Ruby Mae looked surprised. Until then, no one had even bothered to ask her permission. "I s'pose. But watch yourself. He's mighty prickly 'round strangers."

"And who wouldn't be?" the man said in a soft, cooing voice as he stepped into the stall. "All this excitement. All these strangers poring over him like a piece of meat."

Mr. Collins reached into his pocket and pulled out three lumps of sugar. Prince gobbled them up hungrily.

"A sweet tooth, like myself," Mr. Collins said. He smiled at Ruby Mae. "I can tell this horse has been very well cared for. Are you the party responsible?"

"Well, me and the preacher," Ruby Mae replied.

"David Grantland." David shook the man's hand. "And this is Miss Christy Huddleston."

148

"A pleasure." Mr. Collins took another bow, then turned to scratch Prince's ear.

"Why, that's just how Prince likes it," Ruby Mae observed.

"He's a fine stallion. Anyone would be proud to own him."

"Do you have a nice place for runnin'?" Ruby Mae asked. "Prince loves to run."

"The finest. And the finest food, and the finest trainers . . . and of course, sugar every day." He paused. "Forgive me if I carry on. It's just that to me, these animals are more than something I own. They're a responsibility—a gift."

"You're goin' to bid on him, then?" Ruby Mae asked.

"It would be an honor."

"And s'posin' . . ." Ruby Mae faltered, "s'posin' you bought him. Would you reckon maybe some o' his old friends could stop by for a visit, now and then?"

"Anytime," Mr. Collins responded.

"You a good rider?"

"At the risk of sounding immodest," Mr. Collins said, "I am the finest equestrian in this part of Tennessee."

"That's mighty fine, but what about *ridin'?*" Ruby Mae demanded. "Me, I can ride Prince bareback over a four-foot fence."

Mr. Collins raised a brow. "Such an imaginative girl. How delightful. Now, if you'll excuse me, I must take a look at the other animals here. Although I'm sure there'll be no comparison to . . . what did you say his name was?"

"Prince," Ruby Mae replied.

"A fitting name."

Ruby Mae watched Mr. Collins stride away. "Prince," she said, "I hate to see you go, boy. But if you have to go, I reckon there's worse places to end up."

❧ Five ❧

"There he is!" Ruby Mae whispered, squeezing Christy's arm. "It's Prince."

Christy watched as a stable hand led the great stallion into the hay-strewn ring. Prince jerked on his lead rope, then reared up onto his hind legs.

"A spirited one, this horse is!" cried the auctioneer, a heavy-set man with a thick white mustache. "A fine start to the auction indeed!"

The crowd murmured appreciatively as Prince circled the ring.

"He's afeared somethin' terrible," Ruby Mae said. "You can see it in his eyes."

"Ruby Mae, maybe we should wait outside," Christy suggested. "It might be easier—"

"You can git if'n you want," Ruby Mae said. "But I want to see who Prince's new owner's a-goin' to be. I owe him that much, I figure."

"It looks like Mr. Collins is planning to bid," David said. "He's sitting down there in the front row. See?"

"I sure do hope so," Ruby Mae said. "At least then we'd be sure Prince would have a good home. You could tell Mr. Collins loves horses. Almost as much as me, I reckon." She stood, craning her neck to get a better view. "What's goin' to happen now, Preacher?"

"From what I understand, the auctioneer will start the bidding soon. This isn't a big, formal livestock auction like the one I've heard they have in Knoxville. The people who are interested in buying an animal just raise their hands and shout their bids."

"We have here a fine Thoroughbred three-year-old," the auctioneer called out in a rasping voice. "He's owned by the mission over in Cutter Gap."

Prince tossed his head defiantly.

"Feisty," the auctioneer added, "but well-trained."

Ruby Mae nudged David. "Thanks to you and me," she said proudly.

"What do I hear for an opening bid?"

Several hands shot up, and instantly wild shouting began. The bids flew back and forth so quickly that Christy couldn't keep track of them.

"I can't understand the auction-man," Ruby Mae complained. "He's cacklin' faster 'n a mad hen."

"Mr. Collins just made another bid," David said.

Ruby Mae squeezed her eyes shut and clasped her hands together tightly. "Dear God, please let it be Mr. Collins who wins," she prayed aloud, "so that Prince can have all the sugar he ever wants forever and ever. Amen."

She opened one eye. "Was that all right for a prayer, Preacher?"

Just then, the auctioneer cried, "Sold! To Mr. Jared Collins of Great Oak Farm. Congratulations, Mr. Collins, on a fine purchase."

David gave Ruby Mae a hug. "It appears it was an acceptable prayer, Ruby Mae."

"You got what you wanted," Christy said. "Feel a little better?"

"This ain't what I want at all," Ruby Mae replied in a soft voice. "But even if I ain't happy, at least maybe Prince can be."

—◆━◆━◆—

When the sale was over, Christy and Ruby Mae decided to go back to the stalls to say farewell to Prince.

"I'll go on ahead to the cashier and collect the money from Prince's sale," David said.

"Let's meet each other outside the main barn."

"Sure you don't want to come?" Christy asked.

"I've already said my goodbyes. It'll hurt too much to do it again," David murmured.

"We'll just be a few minutes," Christy promised.

"The preacher loves that horse more'n I reckoned," Ruby Mae said as she and Christy made their way through the crowd.

"Yes, he really does."

"I figured . . . I mean, since he was so set on sellin' Prince and all. . . . Well, I guess I figured he didn't care 'bout him like some of us do."

"David loves that horse as much as you do, Ruby Mae. He's just trying to do what's right for the mission."

Prince was stomping around in his stall, tossing his head anxiously. When he caught sight of Ruby Mae, he whinnied softly.

Without another word, Ruby Mae hurried to Prince's stall. Instantly the big horse calmed.

"It's goin' to be all right, boy," she soothed. "You're goin' to be livin' in the finest place around. With all the sugar you can eat."

"This 'un was yours?" asked a gruff older man carrying a new leather bridle.

"Yes," Christy answered. "His name is Prince."

"I'm Uriah Wynne." He gave a terse nod. "Seein' as you know him, maybe you can get this bridle on him. Swear he nearly bit my head off when I tried."

"He's just nervous," Ruby Mae said. "Wouldn't you be, with all these new folks and funny smells?"

"Here." The man thrust the bridle into Ruby Mae's hand. "I'd be much obliged."

"But Prince has already got himself a home-made bridle," Ruby Mae objected.

The man spit on the ground. "I'm just doin' what Mr. C said. Gimme a hand, huh?"

Speaking in low tones to Prince, Ruby Mae quickly removed Lundy's bridle. She handed it to Christy, then dutifully put on the new one. She was just finishing when Mr. Collins strode up.

"Cost me more than I bargained for, but he'll be worth it," he said, "once we get him under control. He's a handful, all right."

"He's awful upset," Ruby Mae said. "Sometimes when he gets like this, it helps if'n you sing 'Amazing Grace' to him. And he loves his new blanket." She pointed to the corner where she'd left the neatly folded blanket. "Me and all my classmates at school, we made it."

"It's certainly . . . colorful. I'll be sure to keep your advice in mind," Mr. Collins said, with a cool smile.

"Mr. Collins, I know this is a great imposition," Christy said, "but one of my students made this bridle for Prince. It would really mean a lot to me if you could take it with him."

"Of course. I'll hang it near his stall, right next to his brass nameplate."

"Thank you so much." Christy turned to Ruby Mae. "Well, I guess it's time to go. We can't delay this forever."

"I know." Ruby Mae rubbed her cheek against Prince's mane. She whispered something to him that no one else could hear. Then, her head held high, she opened the stall door. "Take good care of him," she said, her voice choked.

Christy touched the stallion's nose. "Goodbye, sweet Prince. We'll miss you, boy."

With a nod to Mr. Collins, she put her hand on Ruby Mae's shoulder, and together they started down the aisle.

"Know what I whispered to him?" Ruby Mae said.

"You don't have to tell me," Christy said. "Not if you don't want to."

"I told him someday, somehow, I'd get him back."

Christy wiped away a tear. There was no point in arguing with Ruby Mae. Let her have her tattered hope. They both knew Prince was gone from their lives forever.

As they left the barn, Christy glanced back over her shoulder. Prince was being led away. Mr. Collins was following behind. He paused to toss something into a crate filled with trash, then continued on, basking in the admiring comments from the crowd.

It took Christy a moment before she realized what he'd thrown away.

"Ruby Mae, there's something I want to check. You run on ahead, all right? There's David, over by the cashier. I'll be there in a moment."

Ruby Mae nodded glumly, lost in her own sadness. "Hurry, though, won't you, Miz Christy? I just want to go home now."

Christy ran down the aisle to the pile of trash. Lundy's bridle lay on top. Next to it was Prince's blanket.

She pulled them from the trash. Carefully, she wrapped her shawl around them and tucked the bundle under her arm. Hopefully, Ruby Mae wouldn't ask any questions.

Christy started to call for Mr. Collins, but he had already vanished from view. Maybe, she thought angrily, it was just as well. There was nothing she could say. Prince was his now, and that was that.

I have a special project for all of you today," Christy announced one gloomy afternoon at school.

A week had passed since Prince's sale—a week of tears, moping, pouting, anger, and resignation. Christy had never seen her class so dejected. Finally, she'd decided it was time to take action.

"We're going to write a letter," Christy said, leaning against her battered old desk. "A real, live letter that we're going to mail this afternoon when Mr. Pentland comes."

"Who we goin' to send it to, Teacher?" asked Little Burl Allen.

"Well, I'll give you some hints." Christy closed the window near her desk. A steady, cold rain had sent a damp chill through the schoolhouse, which also doubled as the church on Sundays. Worse yet, one corner of the roof had developed a small, but steady leak.

"He can't read—not yet, anyway. He's very proud. He's a good friend of ours. And—oh, yes—did I mention that he has four legs and a tail?"

"Prince!" Little Burl screeched, as the other students broke into applause.

"Exactly. I thought we'd write him a letter telling him how much we miss him," Christy said. "Of course, we can't afford to send seventy letters. But you each can write one line. That should only take up a couple of pages. Then we'll send that along with Mr. Pentland to the farm where Prince lives."

Ruby Mae's hand shot up. "I don't rightly see the point, if'n you don't mind my sayin' so. I mean, it's like you said yourself, Miz Christy. Prince can't exactly read." She shrugged. "Who knows? Mr. Collins might even just throw the letter away."

Instantly, Christy thought back to the blanket and bridle she'd rescued from the trash heap the day of the auction. Fortunately, she'd managed to keep Mr. Collins' thoughtless act from Ruby Mae. When they'd arrived home that evening, Christy had hidden the items in the trunk in her bedroom.

"This letter isn't so much for Prince as it is for all of us, Ruby Mae," Christy explained. "I

160

think we've all been feeling sad since Prince's sale. And sometimes it helps to write down your feelings."

"Are you sad, Teacher?" Creed asked.

"Very sad, Creed," Christy answered truthfully.

"Don't know why," Ruby Mae muttered. "You got your money, after all."

"It's true, the mission has been able to buy badly needed medicine and supplies. But that doesn't mean I don't miss Prince."

Christy retrieved two precious pieces of paper from her desk. "I'll start the letter," she said. In her careful penmanship, she wrote at the top of the page:

Dear Prince,
    I miss seeing you run in the morning mist. I hope you are happy and eating lots of clover.
                              Miss Huddleston

She held up the paper. "I want each of you to write down a small note just like this, then sign your name. The older students can help the younger ones if they have trouble."

Christy passed the page to Creed. "While Creed writes his letter to Prince, the rest of you can go on with your lessons."

During the morning, the children worked

on their letter. At first they were very quiet, but soon, as Christy had hoped, they began to exchange happy memories about Prince. The conversation grew more animated, and even though a few tears fell, there was plenty of laughter, too. All in all, Christy decided, her idea was a success. At least she'd given the children an opportunity to express their sadness, and that was a start.

After school let out for the day, Christy sat alone at her desk. After addressing the envelope, she re-read the letter the children had composed. Some of the entries made her laugh out loud. Others made her heart ache:

I miss the way you flik off fliz with yer tal.
Creed Allen

Ridin on yoo, I felt jest lik a hawk in the sky.
Wanda Beck

I miss your wild beauty as you ran through the fields.
Rob Allen

Yer eazee to talk 2.
Mountie O'Teale

I mis the wa yu lovd everbodee. Even me.
Lundy Taylor

Even Ruby Mae had relented and added a note, although hers was very brief:

I love you.
Ruby Mae

Well, Christy thought as she folded up the letter and placed it in the envelope, *their spelling needs plenty of work, but not their hearts.*

"Howdy, Miz Huddleston." Ben Pentland, the mailman, appeared in the doorway, dripping wet.

"Mr. Pentland! Come on in and dry yourself off. You must be freezing."

The tall, weathered man removed his hat and stepped inside the schoolroom. He had a long, slim face, creased by wind and weather, and bushy eyebrows that arched above deepset eyes. Carefully, he set down his mailbag.

"I've got a letter for you, Miz Huddleston, all the way from Asheville." He fished inside the bag, then handed an ivory envelope to Christy.

"It's from my mother," she said, smiling at the curly handwriting. "And as it happens, I have a letter for you."

Mr. Pentland examined the address. "But . . . I don't mean to pry, Miz Huddleston, but ain't this letter to a . . . well, a *horse?*"

"The children miss Prince so much. I know it seems silly, but I thought perhaps if we

163

wrote him, it would ease their pain a little. Can it be delivered?"

"Sure can. The U-nited States Postal Service aims to please. I'll make sure that letter gets delivered." His eyes twinkled. "'Course, I can't guarantee it'll get *read,* mind you."

"Thank you, Mr. Pentland." Christy hesitated. "Do you know anything about the folks at Great Oak Farm?"

The mailman shrugged. "It's a fancy enough place. 'Course, I don't deliver mail thataways, but I know the fella who does. Hank Drew's his name."

"Maybe you could ask him . . . I mean, if it's no trouble—"

"To check up on ol' Prince? I'd be happy to. Hank's a bit of a busybody, anyway."

"Thank you. It'd be nice, just to know how things are going."

"You frettin' about Prince's new owner?"

"I'm sure Mr. Collins is a fine man," Christy said. "It's just that I want to be sure Prince is adjusting to his new life. That's all. To put the children's minds at ease."

And my own, she added silently.

❧ Seven ❧

That evening, Christy sat in the mission parlor by a crackling fire and began to write in her diary. She'd filled the pages with her hopes and fears, her embarrassing moments, and her happy ones. Writing down her feelings helped her understand what was happening in her life—the same thing she'd hoped to accomplish today by having the children write a letter to Prince.

Tonight, Prince was very much in her thoughts:

I'm not sure why I can't get that image of Mr. Collins out of my mind—the memory of him tossing aside the blanket and bridle. He's a wealthy man, after all. Perhaps he couldn't see the point in keeping the children's handiwork. To me, those items

*are worth more than all the riches a man like Mr.
Collins possesses, because they're gifts from the heart.*

*What troubles me most was that he'd promised
he would take the items. Was he lying? Or was he
just trying to be kind to Ruby Mae? Perhaps, when
we were gone, he figured there would be no harm in
getting rid of the blanket and bridle. After all, he
probably assumed he'd never see us again.*

*Maybe I'm making too much of this. He was
very kind to Prince and Ruby Mae before that. It's
just that there was something about his smile . . .
something insincere.*

*Listen to me. I'm letting my imagination get
carried away again! Sometimes I think I should be
a writer instead of a teacher, the way I'm always
making up stories.*

Christy paused when she heard someone
come into the parlor.

"Am I interruptin'?" Ruby Mae asked. She
was dressed in her flannel nightgown and
wearing a pair of floppy, hand-me-down
socks.

"Not at all. I'd be glad for the company."

"What you writin'?"

"Actually, I was just writing about Prince. I
miss him a lot."

Ruby Mae sat next to Christy on the sofa.
"Me too. Does the hurtin' ever get any easier,
Miz Christy?"

"Time's a great healer. You'll see."

"Maybe." Ruby Mae didn't sound convinced. "It just seems like sometimes I can't get my mind off him. You know?"

"I have an idea." Christy set her diary aside. From her skirt pocket, she retrieved the letter from her mother. She passed the crisp envelope to Ruby Mae. "This is a letter from my mother that Mr. Pentland brought today. I was saving it to read this evening. Why don't you open it, and we'll read it together?"

"Me?" Ruby Mae's eyes glowed. "Open a real, for-true letter?"

"You can read it out loud. It'll be good practice."

Ruby Mae ran her finger over the sealing wax on the back of the letter, embossed with the letter *H*. "Is *H* for Huddleston?"

"That's right. Just slip your fingernail under the seal and the envelope will open."

"Oh, but I just can't, Miz Christy. It's way too purty."

"Go ahead, Ruby Mae. How else will I know what the letter says?"

"When we're done, can I keep the envelope for my own?"

"Sure."

Slowly, carefully, Ruby opened the envelope and withdrew a piece of thick, ivory stationery.

"Look at how purty your ma writes!" Ruby

167

Mae exclaimed. "All those curlicues like a piglet's tail!"

"I know you're just starting to learn to read cursive writing," Christy said. "Whenever you come to a word you can't figure out, you just tell me."

Ruby Mae cleared her throat and sat up very straight. "'Dearest Christy,'" she began. She grinned. "Guess your ma don't have no cause to call you *Miz.*"

Again she cleared her throat. "'I can't tell you how much your feather and I—'"

"That's probably *father*, Ruby Mae."

"Oops. Yes'm. I do believe it is. Less'n your ma's married to a feather duster." Ruby Mae took a deep breath.

"'—how much your father and I miss you, even after these many months. I find myself talking about you every chance I get. Why, just last Sunday at church, I was telling the editor of the *Asheville C—*'" Ruby Mae frowned. "*C—C—*"

"Sound it out," Christy advised.

"Cou . . . cuckoo?" Ruby asked hopefully.

"*Courier*. It's the Asheville newspaper."

"'I was telling the editor of the *Asheville Courier* all about your adventures, and the interesting people you've met.'"

Ruby Mae glanced at Christy. "Do you ever talk about me, Miz Christy?"

"Of course. You're one of Cutter Gap's most interesting characters."

"How about that! Me, a character!"

"Ruby Mae—the letter."

"Oh. I plumb forgot. Let's see . . . 'He said he'd love to do an article about you, but Cutter Gap is so re . . . remote . . . he just couldn't afford to send a reporter. So I suggested you become a reporter for him and send him articles about your life in Cutter Gap, since you're such a fine writer. And he thought it was a splendid idea.'"

Ruby Mae gasped. "Miz Christy! You could write stories about us for a real newspaper! Wouldn't that just be amazin'? Why, we'd be famous!"

"Oh, I couldn't," Christy protested. "I mean, I'm a teacher, not a writer."

"You write things in your diary most every day."

"But that's different. That's just for me. Besides, who would want to read about my life in Cutter Gap?"

Ruby Mae looked crestfallen. "I s'pose you're right. Those rich people in Asheville don't give a hoot about folks like us."

"Oh, Ruby Mae. That's not what I meant at all!" Christy cried. "It's just that I'm no reporter. I wouldn't know how to describe my life here. I wouldn't be able to do it justice."

"I know what you mean," Ruby Mae said quietly. "It's like today, when you asked us to write Prince how we was feelin'. I thought and thought, but I just couldn't find the right words."

"But you did. You wrote exactly the right words. Three of them, to be exact."

"So how come you couldn't do it, too?"

"This is different. The paper's going to want more than three words."

"So fancy 'em up a bit."

Christy shook her head. "I don't think so, Ruby Mae."

"Fine. Guess I won't get to be famous, after all."

"Oh, I have no doubt you'll be famous someday, Ruby Mae," Christy smiled, "but there's plenty of time for that."

❧ Eight ❧

Three weeks after Prince's sale, Mr. Pentland came to the door of the mission house. "Special delivery from the U-nited States Postal Service!"

"Mr. Pentland," Christy cried, "look at all these boxes! What have you brought us?"

He pointed to the load of crates on his small wagon. "Looks like supplies, unless I miss my guess. All I can tell you is some of them is right heavy."

Miss Alice, David, and Miss Ida came to the door. "My, you *are* a welcome sight, Ben Pentland!" Miss Ida exclaimed.

Mr. Pentland blushed. "Just doin' my job, ma'am."

"We have Prince to thank for this bounty," Miss Alice said.

"Without that money, we wouldn't have been able to buy these supplies."

"That reminds me, Mr. Pentland," Christy said. "Do you know if the children's letter to Prince was safely delivered? It's only been about two weeks since we sent it, but still, I was hoping for a reply of some kind."

David winked at Christy. "He's a fine horse," he said, "but as far as I know, his penmanship is lousy."

"I *meant* from Mr. Collins," Christy said, grinning. "Of course, he's probably too busy . . ."

"There's somethin' I need to be tellin' you folks, much as it pains me," Mr. Pentland said. He hefted a crate off the cart and set it on the ground, then paused.

"What is it, Mr. Pentland?" Christy asked.

The mailman stroked his chin. "Guess there ain't any good way to say this. I ran into Hank Drew yesterday mornin' over at the general store in El Pano. He's the one I told you about, Miz Huddleston, the mailman over to those parts."

"The one who delivers mail to Great Oak Farm?" Christy asked.

"Yep. I asked Hank about the letter to Prince, seein' as how it was a mighty unusual piece o' deliverin'. I've delivered plenty of mail in my time, but I can tell you for sure and certain I ain't never delivered mail to no horse! To any critter, come to think of it."

Christy nodded patiently. Mr. Pentland didn't talk much, but when he did, he had a slow, deliberate way of getting to the point.

"Anyways, Hank and me got to talkin', and he said he gave one of the stable hands—Uriah was his name, I think—the letter." Mr. Pentland offered Christy an apologetic look. "This Uriah fella just up and laughed and crumpled the letter up in a ball. Said maybe Prince'd want to eat it."

"Well, I suppose I should have expected that," Christy said sadly. "After all, the point of the letter was to make the children feel better."

Mr. Pentland cleared his throat. "Thing is, that ain't the whole of it, Miz Huddleston. Seems Uriah told Hank that Prince has been nothin' but trouble since the day they bought him. Ran away twice, he said."

"I'm not really surprised," David said grimly. "Prince always has had a mind of his own."

"It'd be bad enough, the runnin' away," Mr. Pentland said. "But Hank told me as he was leavin', he heard the sound of a whip, crackin' away like thunder. A man was screamin' and carryin' on. And a frightened horse was stomping and whinnying something fierce." He shook his head. "It was Prince. One of the stable hands was beatin' him like there was no tomorrow."

"Oh, no!" Christy cried.

David clenched his fists in fury. "I'll . . . I'll go straight to that Collins, and I'll give him a piece of my mind. Why, I ought to—"

"David," Miss Alice interrupted, "calm down. We're all upset to hear that Prince is being treated badly. But uttering idle threats isn't going to help."

"They *aren't* idle!" David shouted. "I've got half a mind to give that man a taste of his own medicine."

"The sad truth is, Jared Collins is Prince's owner," Miss Alice said. "There's not a whole lot we can do about this. Except, perhaps, to appeal to Mr. Collins' better nature."

"You're going to try to reason with him?" David demanded. "A lot of good that will do. You can't reason with a man like that."

"Perhaps Mr. Collins doesn't know about the way the stable hands are treating Prince," Miss Alice suggested. "Right now, we're leaping to conclusions."

"I'm not so sure, Miss Alice," Christy said. "Maybe I should have seen this coming."

"You?" she asked. "Why?"

"Right after we sold Prince, I saw Mr. Collins throw away Lundy's bridle and the blanket the children made for Prince. I went back and saved them." Christy shook her head. "I know Mr. Collins is a wealthy man and those things must have seemed very crude to him, but there was something so . . . cruel and callous about the way he tossed them aside. It made me worry at the time. Now I see that I should have worried more."

"All the more reason for me to confront him, man to man," David said, his jaw clenched.

Miss Alice put a calming hand on David's shoulder. "David, you know that I, as a Quaker, believe in non-violence. You also know that one of the first things I did when I came to Cutter Gap was buy a gun and learn to shoot it." She chuckled. "No doubt I've had my dear ancestors spinning in their graves ever since."

"Well, I've never seen a better time to use a gun than now," David snapped.

"I'm a better shot than a lot of men in this Cove. And because they know it and respect it, it's given me a base for talking straight to them," Miss Alice said. "But now that I've lived here a while and seen violence close up, I believe in non-violence more than ever."

"Miss Alice is right, David," Christy said. "Threatening Mr. Collins won't help. According to the law, Prince belongs to him."

"So that gives him the right to harm a beautiful, living creature? What about God's law?"

His question hung in the air. "I don't have an easy answer, David," Miss Alice finally said. "But I'll be heading over toward El Pano at the end of the week to check on Kettie Weller's new twins. Why don't I pay Mr. Collins a visit and see what can be done for Prince?"

David frowned. "If it's all the same to you, Miss Alice, I'd rather go myself."

"I don't think that's a good idea," she replied. "You're too upset about this right now. Besides, you've got your work cut out for you here, fixing that leak in the schoolhouse roof."

"I'd like to go along," Christy volunteered. "That is, if David doesn't mind watching the children that day."

"Go ahead," David said resignedly. "Miss Alice is right. The way I feel right now, I'd probably do more harm than good." He gave a self-conscious smile. "Look at me! Some minister, huh? I get angry about something, and my first reaction is to lash out."

"You're only human, David," Christy said.

"Then it's settled," Miss Alice said. "We'll talk to Mr. Collins and see what happens. All we can do is take this one step at a time."

"And in the meantime," David said darkly, "Prince is the one who suffers."

❧ Nine ❧

W hat are you going to say to Mr. Collins when we get there?" Christy asked Miss Alice later that week.

They were almost to Great Oak Farm. The day was overcast and damp, and Christy's legs ached from the long walk to El Pano. They'd taken turns riding Goldie, Miss Alice's horse, and last night they'd rested at Kettie Weller's cabin, but it was still an exhausting trip. Nonetheless, Christy was glad she'd come. Somehow, she felt she owed this much to Prince.

"I'm not sure what I'll say to Mr. Collins," Miss Alice said, bending down to pat Goldie's glistening mane. "But I'm sure the Lord will help me find the words."

"You always do seem to know just the right thing to say. I'll bet you would have made a fine writer, Miss Alice," Christy smiled, ". . . or a preacher."

"I wouldn't have the patience to put words on paper," Miss Alice replied. "And as for preaching, I'm ministering the way I love best—doing a little bit of everything. Teaching, doctoring, you name it. I suppose you could say I'm a jack-of-all-trades."

Christy lifted her long skirt to step over a fallen log. "You know, I got a letter from my mother not long ago. She said the editor of the newspaper back home in Asheville had suggested I write about my experiences here in Cutter Gap."

"And what was your response?"

"I told her to tell him I was flattered, but that I didn't think I'd be very good at it."

Miss Alice shook a finger at Christy. "You'd be good at anything you set your mind to, Christy Huddleston. I truly believe that." She paused. "Although in this case, you probably made the right decision. The people of Cutter Gap are a proud lot— proud and terribly private. I'm not sure how they'd take to the notion of your writing about them."

"I tried to start an article," Christy admitted. "You know—just to see if I could do it." She shrugged. "Actually, I was just writing in my diary, and it sort of turned into a piece about Prince, and all he'd meant to the children. But after everything that happened with him, I couldn't find the heart to finish it."

They came to a fork in the path. On the right, the path broadened into a wide, dirt road. "Another half-mile or so up that road, and we'll be to Great Oak Farm," Christy said.

"You know, I'd like to read that story about Prince sometime, if you feel like sharing it," Miss Alice said.

"I'll think about it. But first, let's see if it's going to have a happy ending."

~ ~ ~

"Well, it's a beautiful farm," Miss Alice said. "I'll give it that much."

Christy surveyed the manicured lawn and immaculate stables. The imposing white house was a few hundred yards from the stables. A broad path lined in stately oaks led to the front porch. "Should we go knock on the front door?"

Miss Alice dismounted and tied Goldie to a nearby tree. "We're here to visit Prince," she said firmly. "Better to arrive unexpected and see how he's doing first. Then we'll say hello to Mr. Collins."

They started for the largest barn. In the fenced-off field in the distance, several beautiful horses grazed contentedly. "They look happy enough," Christy whispered to Miss Alice. "Maybe Mr. Pentland's friend was wrong. Maybe this is all some terrible mistake." But even to her own ears, her words sounded hollow.

The barn was cool and quiet, filled with the sweet scent of hay. Most of the stalls were empty, and there were no stable hands in sight. Christy and Miss Alice walked slowly down the aisle, taking in the brass name plates on the door. *Rebel. Jericho. Long Shot.*

And then, there it was: *Prince.*

Christy ran her fingers over the engraved name. Suddenly, a terrible noise met her ears—the heart-breaking sound of an animal in pain.

"Prince!" Christy cried. "That's him, I know it is!"

She ran down the aisle to the end of the barn, with Miss Alice close on her heels. At the open door, they stopped short.

In a nearby paddock stood four men. Prince was in the middle of the paddock. His mouth was foaming. His coat was slick with sweat.

"Told you he can't be ridden." One of the men spat in disgust. "If I didn't know better, I'd swear he ain't saddle-broke."

"I'll show him who's boss," another man said.

Christy grabbed Miss Alice's arm. "That's

Uriah Wynne," she said, "the stable hand at the auction."

Uriah grabbed a whip and coiled it in his right hand. Slowly he approached Prince, talking to him under his breath. "You better mind me, boy, or you'll be worm food before I'm through with you," he muttered.

With each step closer, Prince grew more agitated. His ears flickered wildly, and his eyes were wide with fear. Suddenly, he reared up, his great hooves flailing in the air, towering over Uriah.

Crack! In a flash, Uriah let loose the whip. It caught Prince on his right shoulder, and the stallion leapt back in shock.

Again Uriah let the leather whip fly. The whip cracked, and the stallion reared up in pain.

"I don't care what it takes," Christy cried in horror. "I've got to find a way to get Prince away from here!"

❧ Ten ❧

Stop it!" Christy screamed, dashing to the fence. "Stop it, now! You're hurting him!"

"Well, looky here," one of the men said. "We got ourselves some lady visitors."

Miss Alice strode up calmly. "Prince," she said in a soothing voice. "Calm down, boy."

Prince lowered his front hooves. He jerked his head in confusion.

Miss Alice clucked her tongue, and in an instant, Prince seemed to recognize her. Slowly, nervously, he approached them. Christy leaned over the fence and embraced his neck while Miss Alice stroked his ears.

"This is a fine horse, gentlemen," Miss Alice said in a stern voice. "But like all animals, he responds better to kindness than to threats."

"Is that so?" Uriah swaggered over, tapping

the whip handle in his palm. "And just who are you to be tellin' us our business, lady?"

"Uriah!" came a sharp voice. "That will be enough."

Striding toward the paddock came Jared Collins. He was wearing a starched white shirt, riding breeches, and tall, black leather riding boots.

With a gracious smile, he bowed low to Christy. "This young lady is Miss Christy Huddleston from the Cutter Gap mission," he said to Uriah, "and to my great delight, our most welcome guest." He turned to Miss Alice. "Jared Collins, at your service. And you might be?"

"Alice Henderson," Miss Alice said coolly.

"How can you sit there introducing yourself like nothing's wrong?" Christy demanded, rounding on Mr. Collins. "Didn't you see? He—he was beating Prince! How can you let someone like this work for you?"

"Uriah is one of my most trusted hands. He's worked with horses since he was just a boy. I'm sure you're misinterpreting events, Miss Huddleston."

"Misinterpreting?" Christy cried in fury. "He beat him with a whip! You could have heard Prince in the next county, he was in so much pain!"

"The use of a whip when training horses is not at all uncommon," Mr. Collins said, favoring Christy with a tolerant smile. "In fact, it's often recommended for a horse with Prince's—shall we say—difficult temperament."

Miss Alice cleared her throat. "Mr. Collins, I can tell you with some authority that Prince does not have a difficult temperament. Quite the contrary. When treated with respect and love, he responds beautifully to commands. Certainly he's strong-willed, but with a knowledgeable rider—"

"I assure you, Madam, I am an accomplished equestrian."

"Then you know," Miss Alice continued in her calm, deliberate way, "that a horse who has learned to fear is a horse who cannot be managed."

"In my experience, fear leads to respect."

"I know ten-year-old girls who can handle that horse better than your men," Miss Alice said, "and they do it with love."

"I own dozens of horses, Madam," Mr. Collins said dismissively. "I don't have time for—" he sneered, "love. Besides, look around you. This is the finest horse farm in seven counties. Prince has everything a stallion could ask for. The finest care, the finest food, the finest pasture."

Christy rubbed her cheek against Prince's hot, damp neck. "All I know is, I've never seen him like this. He's afraid. He's unhappy."

"He's merely untrained and ill-mannered,"

Mr. Collins said. "When a horse won't respond to a rider of my impeccable training, the problem, dear lady, lies with the horse."

For a moment, no one spoke. Uriah spat on the ground. Far off in the distance, a horse whinnied softly.

"Mr. Collins," Miss Alice said at last, "we may differ on how to care for a horse like Prince. But there's one thing I think we can agree on—he's a fine animal."

"Indeed. On that we do agree."

"Perhaps you're right, and the problem lies in the way Prince has been trained. If that's the case, we both know it's probably too late to change him. Suppose we agree that things haven't worked out? The mission will take him off your hands, and return your money in full as soon as we can manage it."

Christy nearly gasped. How could Miss Alice make such an offer? Where would the mission ever get the money to repay Mr. Collins?

Mr. Collins tried to pat Prince on the shoulder, but the horse moved out of his reach. "Thank you for your offer, Miss Henderson. It's very generous of you. But this horse belongs to me, and I intend to keep him. As a matter of fact, I intend to be riding him before the month is out." He gave an icy smile. "Perhaps I'll ride by your dark little corner of the world and show you how it's done. It's really very simple. With a dumb animal like this, you just have to show him who's boss." He bowed. "Now, if you'll excuse me, I have other matters to attend to. I'm sure you can find your way out."

⌇ ⌇ ⌇

"I still can't believe you offered to buy Prince back," Christy said that afternoon as she and Miss Alice headed back to Cutter Gap.

Miss Alice sighed. "It was worth a try."

"But where would we have found the money?"

"The Lord has a way of providing."

"Did you—" Christy glanced over her shoulder. "Did you hear something just now? Behind us, I mean?"

"You're just tired. Why don't you ride Goldie for a while? It's your turn."

"I'm fine. I just thought I heard someone following us." Christy shook her head. "Every time I close my eyes, I hear Prince crying out in pain. Miss Alice, isn't there something else we can do?"

"I gave Mr. Collins our address," Miss Alice reminded her, "and I told him to contact us immediately if he decides Prince is too much trouble. I don't know what we can do beyond that."

"It's so unfair," Christy groaned. "Owning an animal doesn't give you a license to mistreat it. I just feel so . . . so hopeless."

"Whatever you do, Christy, you must never give up hope." Miss Alice looked down at her with her warm, tender gaze, and somehow Christy felt better. "For now, we'll pray for Prince's well-being, and that God will provide a way for us to solve this problem. In the meantime, promise me you won't stop hoping. Who knows what tomorrow may bring?"

❧ Eleven ❧

That night, Christy lay in her bed, exhausted, sore, and dejected.

She had blisters on both her feet. Her leg muscles had turned to hard knots. Her face was chapped from the cold, wet air. But it was her heart that was truly hurting.

She opened her diary and stared at the single sentence she'd written after coming home:

How could we have abandoned Prince?

But of course, they'd had no choice. Prince belonged to Mr. Collins, and that was that.

Perhaps they could have gone to the local sheriff and complained about Prince's mistreatment. But Christy knew that would have been pointless. These mountains were ruled by guns. This was a place where women and children could be horribly mistreated, and no one—not even the law—would lift a finger to help them. Nobody in these parts had the time to worry about a mistreated horse. Especially when the horse was living at Great Oak Farm, the finest farm for miles around.

Christy turned to the story about Prince that she'd mentioned to Miss Alice. It began:

He's just a horse, some would say. Four sturdy legs. A shiny mane. An insatiable taste for sugar.

But I know better. I've seen the little miracles.

Around Prince, the little girl who stutters somehow speaks with ease.

Around Prince, the vicious bully turns gentle and protective.

Around Prince, the child set apart by the color of her skin becomes a friend at last.

He may be just a horse, but try telling that to my seventy Cutter Gap students.

With a heavy sigh, Christy closed her diary. There was no point in reading on. Prince's story did not have a happy ending, after all.

Christy put out the light and closed her

eyes. But every time she started to drift off, she imagined she could hear Prince. Sometimes it was just his familiar, soft nicker. Other times it was the horrifying whinny of terror and pain she'd heard today at the farm.

Soon another noise drifted into her awareness. *Tap, tap, tap.*

"Miz Christy?"

The muffled voice had to belong to Ruby Mae. Christy climbed out of bed, threw on her robe to ward off the chill, and opened the door.

Ruby Mae was standing in the dark hallway. Her face was in shadow, but there was just enough moonlight spilling from Christy's window to illuminate Ruby Mae's huge grin.

"I got a surprise for you," Ruby Mae said. She was wearing her worn, wool coat over her nightgown. Her feet were bare.

"It had better be a good surprise, at this time of night," Christy replied.

"I'll give you some hints," Ruby Mae whispered loudly. "He can't read—not yet, anyway. He's very proud. He's a good friend of ours. Let's see what else. Oops. Almost forgot. He's got four legs and a mighty fine tail."

Christy grabbed Ruby Mae by the shoulders and pulled her into the room. "Ruby Mae, I want you to wake up," she commanded. "I think you're sleepwalking."

Ruby Mae leapt onto Christy's bed, laughing gaily. "Not hardly." She pinched her arm. "See? I'm as awake as can be, Miz Christy."

"All right. Start over. Tell me exactly what you're talking about," Christy said as she lit her lamp.

"You won't believe me even if I tell you. How about I *show* you what I'm talkin' about? Then you'll know I ain't a-dreamin'."

Christy put on her slippers. "Fine, then. You can show me. But after that, you're going straight to bed so you can finish this nice dream—or whatever it is."

Ruby Mae grabbed Christy's hand and led her down the staircase. The mission house was still, except for the soft sound of snoring drifting down from Miss Ida's room.

Outside, the wind was brisk and the sky was crowded with dazzling stars. "Shouldn't you go put on some shoes?" Christy asked, hesitating on the porch.

"I'm so excited I can't feel a thing!" Ruby Mae exclaimed. "Come on, Miz Christy! Hurry!"

Ruby Mae dashed across the dark lawn toward the little stable that housed the mission's animals. It was just an overgrown shed that David had built with bits and pieces of leftover lumber, but at least it provided shelter from the weather.

Shivering, Christy hurried toward the stable.

When she was closer, she could hear Ruby Mae chattering away inside.

"Ruby Mae, I really wish you'd tell me what this is about," Christy said as she reached the doorway. But even before she'd spoken the words, she had her answer.

"Prince!" Christy gasped.

"Told you! Ain't it a plumb fine miracle, Miz Christy?" Ruby Mae said, beaming. She planted a kiss on Prince's nose. He responded with a polite attempt to eat her hair.

"But . . . but how . . ."

"All I know is, I was havin' a wonderful dream that Prince had come back. All of a sudden I clean woke up, and sure as shootin', I coulda swore I heard him nickerin' below my window. So I went and looked, and who do you think I saw?"

Christy scratched the great stallion's ear. "He must have found his way home. You know, I *thought* I heard someone following us on our way back from Mr. Collins'. You don't think he escaped from Great Oak Farm and followed us, do you?"

"Prince is smarter than a whole passel o' humans. I wouldn't be surprised if you told me he could recite the alphabet backwards."

Christy laughed, but Ruby Mae's expression grew grave. "Miz Christy, you ain't a-goin' to make him go back, are you? He come all this way 'cause it's us he wants to be with."

"He belongs to Mr. Collins, Ruby Mae. I don't see how we can keep him."

But I don't see how we can send him back, either, she added silently. *Not after what Miss Alice and I saw today.*

Ruby Mae thought for a while. "I'm stayin' with him tonight. Could be it's the last night Prince'll be here."

"Ruby Mae, you can't. You'll catch cold out here. It's freezing."

"I'm stayin', and that's all there is to it."

Christy knew all too well the determined look on Ruby Mae's face. She also knew it was pointless to argue with her.

"I'll go get some blankets and some warm clothes for both of us," Christy said at last.

"Both of us?"

"I'm not letting you stay out here by your-self, Ruby Mae." Christy smiled at Prince. "After all, he's my friend, too."

✒ Twelve ✒

Have you ever seen them so happy?" Christy asked the next day.

Christy, David, and Miss Alice were standing in the yard outside the schoolhouse during the noon break. Nearby, Ruby Mae and Hannah were leading Prince in slow circles, giving rides to the younger children.

"It's like a party," David agreed, "and look at Prince. You can tell he loves being the center of attention again."

Miss Alice shook her head. "I still can't believe he found his way home. It's quite amazing."

They watched as Prince came to a halt. Carefully, Ruby Mae helped Little Burl down off the stallion. Mountie, who was next in line for a ride, smiled gleefully as Hannah helped her aboard Prince's broad back.

"I missed you, Prince," Mountie said in a clear, joyful voice. "I sure am glad you decided to come visit for a spell."

Christy glanced at David, then looked away. That, of course, was the question—how long would Prince be a part of their lives this time?

"I don't see how we can take him back to Great Oak," David said, "knowing what we know. It just wouldn't be fair."

"He doesn't belong to us, David," Miss Alice reminded him. "He's still the property of Jared Collins."

"Maybe if we just stall for a while," Christy suggested. "We might come up with a solution, if we just give it some time. At least—" she lowered her voice as some of the children ran past, "at least we'll know Prince is safe, for the time being."

Miss Alice leaned against an oak tree, watching Hannah lead Prince around the yard. "Stalling is hardly a solution," she said.

"I know," Christy sighed. "But what else *can* we do?"

"I'll tell you one thing," David said firmly. "I am not going to be part of any decision to send Prince back to Great Oak Farm. When I think of him being whipped and abused, it just makes my blood boil—"

"David. Shh." Christy grabbed his arm. "Ruby Mae is coming—"

"Hello, Ruby Mae," David said cheerfully, spinning around to greet her, "and what can we do for you?"

Ruby Mae cocked her head to one side, eyeing him doubtfully. "Who got whopped?"

"Ruby Mae, that conversation was between David and Miss Alice and me," Christy interjected. "You have no right to be eavesdropping."

But Ruby Mae was determined. "This is about Prince, ain't it?" she demanded, her expression hardening. "He done got hisself whopped over at Great Oak, didn't he?"

"This doesn't concern you, Ruby Mae," David said wearily.

Ruby Mae planted her hands on her hips. "Was they treatin' him bad over at that fancy farm?" she cried. "I'll bet that's how come he run away!" She frowned at Christy. "We stayed with him all last night, and you didn't even tell me! And you call yourself his friend?"

Christy rubbed her eyes. "There wasn't any point in worrying you, Ruby Mae. And it doesn't seem like there's anything we can do. Prince belongs to Mr. Collins—"

"So that makes it all right to hurt him?"

"No, of course not. But—"

"So what are you plannin' now? You goin' to give him back, like a cup o' sugar you borrowed? Send him back to those bad people like nothin's wrong?"

Ruby Mae didn't wait for an answer. She stomped off across the lawn, her red hair flying.

"So what *are* we planning?" David asked softly.

Christy shrugged. "Let's just say we're hoping for divine guidance. The sooner, the better."

———

That night, Christy awoke to the sound of the downstairs door closing. She sat up in bed, alert and listening. Were those footsteps she'd heard, or was it just the wind?

Cautiously, she tiptoed down the stairway. Her lamp spread a golden glow over the dark house.

"Miss Ida?" she asked, but the only answer was the sound of a branch creaking outside.

Christy checked the door and scanned the parlor. Nothing. With a sigh, she headed back upstairs. She was probably just imagining things. Of course, last night Ruby Mae had imagined that she'd heard a horse outside her window—and she'd been right!

When she passed Ruby Mae's door, Christy peeked inside. Ruby Mae was sound asleep, snoring softly and looking angelic. Christy smiled. Children always looked so peaceful and innocent when they were asleep.

Quietly, Christy closed Ruby Mae's door.

It was a shame Ruby Mae had overheard David's comment today. There was no point whatsoever in worrying the children about Prince. They had enough pain to deal with every day.

It wasn't until she was climbing into bed that Christy realized something hadn't quite been right with the angelic impression she'd had of Ruby Mae. Was she imagining things, or had one of Ruby Mae's feet been sticking out from the covers—and wearing a *shoe?*

Curious, Christy returned to Ruby Mae's room and cracked open the door.

Ruby Mae's shoes were on the floor. Both of them.

Christy yawned. Once again, her imagination was getting the better of her.

≈ Thirteen ≈

He's gone," David said the next morning when Christy came downstairs.

Christy blinked, taking in the scene in the dining room. David was sitting at the table with Miss Ida and Miss Alice. All of them looked grim. Apparently, Ruby Mae wasn't awake yet.

"Who's gone?" Christy asked, but the look on David's face told her all she needed to know.

"Prince." David combed fingers through his tousled hair. "Vanished, without a trace. I followed some tracks, but I lost them in the woods after about a quarter-mile."

Christy took a seat at the table. "What do you think happened?"

"Could be he ran away, but I doubt it. The latch on his stall was secure last night. I checked it before I went to bed."

Miss Ida poured Christy a cup of tea. "Maybe that awful Mr. Collins tracked him down and took Prince back."

"It's possible," Miss Alice said, "but in the middle of the night?"

"Besides, if Collins had found Prince here, he would have confronted us about it, I'd think." David leaned back in his chair, arms crossed over his chest. "Of course, there are other possibilities."

"Do you mean that terrible Lyle Duster and his brother Ed might have stolen Prince?"

David looked surprised, then thoughtful. "That's always a possibility," he admitted. "Actually, I was thinking that our problem may lie closer to home. Somebody who loves Prince may have hidden him to protect him," David replied.

Just then, Ruby Mae sauntered down the stairs. She yawned, stretched her arms out over her head, and grinned. "Mornin'. Everybody sleep all right?"

"Actually," Christy said, "I had some trouble sleeping. I thought I heard someone come into the house late last night, so I came downstairs to check."

"Probably just the wind," Ruby Mae said, looking away. She reached for a piece of toast and took her seat next to Christy. "It was mighty windy last night."

"Oh?" Christy asked. "Were you up, too?"

"Me? I just got woke up by the wind noise, same as you. Only for a minute. The rest o' the night, I slept just like a babe."

Everyone watched in silence as Ruby Mae gobbled down her toast and reached for another piece.

"What?" she demanded. "Why in tarnation is everybody starin' at me? Was I talkin' with my mouth full again?"

"Ruby Mae," Miss Alice said, "Prince is missing."

Ruby Mae's jaw went slack. She dropped her toast into her lap. "You mean—you mean they done took him back?"

"We're not sure *what* to think," Christy said. "Do you have any idea what might have happened to him?"

"Well . . ." Ruby Mae retrieved her toast and took a bite while she considered the question. "I s'pose he coulda run back to Great Oak all on his own, but that don't seem likely."

"No," David agreed, "it doesn't."

"Or them awful, sneaky men at the auction could o' made off with him." David and Christy exchanged glances.

"Or," Ruby Mae continued, "he could be hidin' somewheres on account o' he's afraid o' goin' back."

"All on his own?" Christy asked.

"You know, Miz Christy, he's a right smart horse."

"Not that smart."

Ruby Mae gulped down the rest of her toast and leapt out of her seat. "Well, I s'pose I ought to be gettin' ready for school. I plumb overslept."

"You know, you don't seem all that upset about Prince's disappearance," David noted.

"Oh, I'm worried, Preacher. But it's like I said—Prince is a right smart horse."

With that, Ruby Mae rushed back up the stairs, taking two steps at a time.

Christy looked at the others. "What do you think?"

"I think," Miss Alice said, "that this problem just keeps getting more and more complicated."

"I think," David added, "that Ruby Mae has great potential as a dramatic actress."

*　～　～　～*

"What are you working on, Christy?" Miss Alice asked early that evening.

They were sitting in the parlor by a crackling fire. Christy was curled up on the worn, old sofa, and Miss Alice was seated across from her, sipping on a cup of tea while she stared out the window at the darkening sky.

Christy held up her diary. "I should be working on my lesson plans. But to tell you the truth, I was writing about Prince in my diary. Sometimes, when I write things down, it helps me clarify my thoughts."

"And this time?"

"This time, I'm afraid it's not helping. Miss Alice, the way the children acted today at school, I'm sure they know what happened to Prince. For one thing, there was far too much whispering and note-passing. For another, they hardly mentioned his disappearance. And as if that weren't enough, they were unusually well-behaved."

"So you think after Ruby Mae overheard David, she decided to kidnap Prince?"

"Horse-nap, is more like it. But I'll bet it wasn't just Ruby Mae. I wouldn't be surprised if several of the children were involved."

"A conspiracy, in our very midst. If you're right, they could have hidden him anywhere. In these mountains, it could take months to find him. Years, even."

"If the children took Prince, I'm sure that's what they're hoping." Christy sighed. "The truth is, I wish I knew for sure they took him. It would certainly be a relief to know that Prince is safe. Of course, it also presents another problem: The children need to learn that they can't go around taking other people's property."

"Christy, you're limited in what you can do until you're sure what's really happened. This is turning into quite a messy story." Miss

Alice pointed to Christy's diary. "You know, speaking of stories, you told me a while ago that you might let me read that article about Prince."

"It still doesn't have an ending. And besides, it's really not very good, Miss Alice."

"Why don't you let me be the judge of that?"

Reluctantly, Christy opened her worn diary to the page where her story about Prince began. She passed the book to Miss Alice.

While the fire crackled away, Miss Alice read, smiling occasionally. When she was done, she closed the diary and wiped away a tear.

"That was lovely, Christy. You truly captured the way Prince changed the children's lives." She paused. "I think I was wrong when I said the folks in Cutter Gap might be offended by an article. Why don't you send this to the editor in Asheville? I'll bet he'd be proud to publish it. And I think the children would be honored to see it in print."

"Oh, Miss Alice, I'm not sure I'd have the nerve. Besides, it doesn't have an ending. We don't even know what's happened to Prince."

"I'm not sure it needs an ending. It's beautiful, just the way it is. This is a story about a group of loving children, and the way their love for an animal helped them through some hard times. Whatever happens with Prince, that won't change."

Christy thumbed through the pages of her diary. "I suppose I could send it in. Who knows—the editor might even pay me something for it. And the Lord knows we could use the money."

"Well, that's one thing settled," Miss Alice said. "Now, if we could just decide what to do about our missing horse."

"Let's give the children some time. I have a feeling they'll tell us the truth eventually."

"Let's hope so."

Christy grinned. "A wise woman once told me never to give up hope."

Miss Alice smiled back. "She was right."

❧ Fourteen ❧

R eady or not, it's time for your spelling test," Christy announced one afternoon.

A week and a half had passed since Prince's disappearance. So far, no one had stepped forward to admit any involvement. In fact, the children hardly mentioned Prince at all—a sure sign, in Christy's mind, that they were keeping a very big secret.

"While the test is going on, I want the younger students to practice writing the alphabet on their chalkboards," Christy instructed. "Are the rest of you ready?"

"Ain't never ready for spellin' tests," Creed muttered.

"Actually, spelling is very important, Creed," Christy said as she erased the chalkboard at the front of the room. "If we can't spell correctly, we can't communicate with each other as efficiently. And communicating with each other is very important." She gave the class a meaningful look. "Even when it's very difficult to do."

She perched on the edge of her battered, wooden desk. "All right, then. Your first word is *prince.*"

A low murmur went through the room, but soon the children were concentrating on their small chalkboards. The only sound was the soft *tap-tap-tap* of the chalk as they wrote.

"The next word is," Christy continued, *"honesty."*

She noticed Ruby Mae and Lundy exchanging a glance before they began writing. A few other students looked a little uncomfortable.

"And your next word is *hiding.*"

Ruby Mae grimaced and raised her hand. "Miz Christy? I got a spellin' question for you," she said in an accusing voice. "How do you spell *whoppin'?*"

The other students nodded in agreement. It was clear everyone understood what Ruby Mae really meant.

"Well, that's a good question, Ruby Mae," Christy said guardedly. "And I—"

"Excuse me for interruptin'," came a gruff voice at the doorway.

It was Uriah Wynne, along with two other

stable hands Christy recognized from Great Oak Farm.

"Mr. Wynne!" Christy cried, her heart leaping into her throat. "This really isn't a good time. As you can see, I'm in the middle of teaching a class."

"This won't take but a minute." Uriah stepped into the classroom, leaving his two friends by the door. "I think you know why we're here. We come for Prince."

"Prince," Christy repeated. She cast a glance at the children. They were sitting erect in their seats, silent as stones.

"We know he come here. Word got back to El Pano. Somebody out thisaways said he come runnin' here."

Christy cleared her throat. "Well, you're right, actually. He did come here. He must have followed Miss Alice and me home."

"Broke outa his pen." Uriah started to spit, then thought better of it. "Confounded horse is more trouble than he's worth, if you ask me. But Mr. C won't give up on him. Don't ask me why. He can't ride him, that's for sure." He rubbed his hands together. "So where is he?"

Christy looked at her students. Their faces were grave. No one said a word. No one moved a muscle.

"I wish I could tell you, Mr. Wynne," Christy said, "but the truth is, Prince disappeared not long after he got here. The Reverend Grantland was able to follow his tracks for about a quarter of a mile, but then he lost them in the woods. We haven't seen him since."

Uriah strode toward Christy, his eyes blazing. "Looky here, little lady. I ain't got time for no games. We been lookin' for this horse for way too long, and Mr. C's like to fire us or worse if'n we don't bring him back."

"I'm telling you the truth, Mr. Wynne," Christy said, "and now, if you please, I'd appreciate it if you'd leave my classroom. We have a spelling test to complete."

"Why, I oughta—" Uriah lifted his arm as if he were going to strike Christy.

Instantly, Lundy leapt from his desk. He grabbed Uriah's arm and easily pinned it behind the man's back. "Don't you be threatenin' Teacher, hear?" he growled.

"Git him offa me!" Uriah groaned.

"Lundy, that's enough," Christy instructed. "You may let Mr. Wynne go now."

Reluctantly, Lundy released the man. "Ain't polite to threaten a lady," he muttered.

Christy almost smiled. It wasn't so long ago that Lundy himself had threatened Christy. She supposed this was progress—of a sort.

"I will pass your concerns along, Mr. Wynne," Christy said. "I'm confident that if anyone in Cutter Gap knows of Prince's whereabouts, they'll inform Mr. Collins."

Uriah narrowed his eyes. "We'll be back," he said, shaking a finger at her. "Mr. C ain't the kind to let somethin' like this go. And believe you me, lady, you don't want to go troublin' Mr. C."

When the men had left, Christy straightened her skirt and forced a smile. "I'm sure you were all hoping I'd forget about the spelling test after that little interruption. I'm afraid you're not going to be that fortunate."

The children didn't respond. They were staring at the doorway where Uriah and his friends had just departed.

"Your next word," Christy said forcefully, "is *secret.*"

"I'm thinkin' on another word—" Ruby Mae muttered softly, *"afeared."*

✒ Fifteen ✒

Howdy, Miz Huddleston!"

Christy peeked past the wet bed sheet she was hanging on the clothesline to dry. "Mr. Pentland! How are you this afternoon? It's nice to see some sun for a change."

"Yes'm. Reckon you're right about that." The mailman reached into his bag. "Got a letter for ya. Don't look like it's from your ma, though. Not, of course, that employees of the U-nited States Postal Service would ever snoop into a person's mail, mind you."

"Of course not." Christy accepted the long, white envelope. It wasn't her mother's stationery, and the ink on the return address was blurred.

She started to open it, then hesitated. Could this be from Mr. Collins? More than a week had passed since Uriah had come to

Cutter Gap. But Christy felt certain that the threatening visit hadn't been the end of things.

"Any sign o' Prince?" Mr. Pentland inquired.

"No. Nothing. Have you heard anything?"

Mr. Pentland shook his head. "Heard some talk about Jared Collins sendin' his men over to these parts."

"Yes. They did pay us a visit."

"I reckon they weren't too friendly, neither."

"That would be a fair statement," Christy said as she removed the letter from its envelope.

"Good news, I hope?" Mr. Pentland asked.

"Oh, my!" Christy scanned the address at the top of the letter. "It's from the *Asheville Courier!* This *is* good news! They want to buy an article I wrote!"

"Well, I'll be. Ain't that somethin'? A real live writer, right here in Cutter Gap."

Christy kissed Mr. Pentland on the cheek. "Thank you, Mr. Pentland. This is wonderful news!"

She left the blushing mailman and ran into the mission house. "Miss Ida! Miss Alice! Ruby Mae! David! Come quickly!"

They all came running. Christy waved her letter in the air triumphantly. "They're going to publish my story about Prince in the Asheville newspaper!"

"Christy, that's wonderful!" David cried, giving her a hug.

"I'm not the least bit surprised," Miss Alice said.

Christy passed the letter to Miss Alice. "See? The editor said my article will bring smiles of joy to his readers. And he's going to pay me, can you believe it? We can use the money for medicine, or maybe some books for the school."

"Miz Christy," Ruby Mae asked, "am I in the story?"

"Yes, you are, as a matter of fact. I talked about how you'd learned to be responsible and disciplined, caring for Prince."

"Me, in a big-city newspaper!" Ruby Mae said, shaking her head. "Imagine that!"

"The editor even asked if I had more stories about Cutter Gap that I wanted to send along," Christy said. "But I'll have to think about that."

Ruby Mae sighed heavily.

"What's wrong, Ruby Mae?" Miss Alice asked.

"Oh, nothin'. I was just a-wishin' Prince could be here to see all the fuss. He's goin' to be famous, and he won't even know it."

"I'm sure he'll hear about it, one way or another," David said with a tolerant smile.

"Maybe," Ruby Mae agreed. "I s'pose anything is possible."

"Miz Christy?" Ruby Mae asked that evening. "You mind some company?"

Christy was sitting in a rocker on the porch, a shawl around her shoulders. "Of course not. Come join me."

"Whatcha doin'?"

"Looking at the stars. And thinking."

"I been thinkin', too," Ruby Mae said. "Which I generally try not to do, what with it makin' my head hurt and all."

"What have you been thinking about, Ruby Mae? Maybe I can help you and your head won't hurt so much."

"Well, first off," Ruby Mae said, rocking back and forth in the chair next to Christy's, "I was thinkin' on how that big-city editor asked you to write more stories for him. Me, I got plenty o' stories about Cutter Gap folks saved up. I could help you out, if'n you got stuck."

"That's a very generous offer, Ruby Mae."

"And then, if you sold him a passel o' stories, you'd make a heap o' money, right?"

"Well, some, anyway."

Ruby Mae paused. "Probably enough so's you could buy Prince back from the mean folks at Great Oak Farm."

"How could we buy him back, Ruby Mae, when we don't even know where he is?"

Ruby Mae cast a nervous look at Christy. "Well, I *meant* s'posin' we found him—you know, way up in the woods somewheres. Then, when you got your money, we could buy him back, right?"

"Well, that presumes a lot. I'm not sure Mr. Collins would be interested in selling Prince."

"Oughta be. That Uriah man said he can't even ride him."

"I would certainly write those articles to help buy Prince back. But you can't buy a horse that isn't there. Besides, it would take a long time to earn enough money to buy Prince."

"Oh." Ruby Mae stopped rocking. She gazed up at the mountains, looming black shadows against a starlit sky. "How do you fight back, Miz Christy? I mean, when you ain't got nothin' to fight with? How do you beat a man like Mr. Collins?"

Christy sighed. "I don't know the answer to that question."

"But you're the teacher. You're *supposed* to know the answer."

"I do know this. It's something Miss Alice told me when I first came to these mountains and I was frightened by all the feuding and violence. She said that evil is real and powerful, and God is against evil all the way. She said we can try to persuade ourselves that evil doesn't exist, or keep quiet about it and say it's none of our business. Or we can work on God's side."

"But how? What if you don't know how?" Ruby Mae asked in a pleading voice.

More clearly than ever, Christy realized that if the children were hiding Prince, it wasn't just a game. They were protecting something they loved in the only way they knew how. Christy and David and Miss Alice knew it wouldn't last forever, that eventually Mr. Collins would track Prince down. But that didn't matter to Ruby Mae and her friends. What mattered to them was that they were fighting evil in the only way they could.

"Even a man like Mr. Collins has weaknesses," Christy said. "Perhaps, if he finds Prince and takes him back, he'll grow bored with him. Perhaps he'll get frustrated and embarrassed when Prince refuses to let him ride."

"Maybe."

"Sometimes even the most complicated story has a happy ending, Ruby Mae. You just have to have faith that with God's help we'll be able to change things."

"I'll try," Ruby Mae said softly. "One thing I *do* know how to do is pray."

Christy smiled. "I can't think of a better time to get in a little practice."

❧ Sixteen ❧

Miz Christy! It's Mr. Collins a-comin'," Ruby Mae called the next day. "And he's brung the sheriff with him!"

It was the noon break, and the children were spread out on the lawn outside the schoolhouse in small groups, eating their meager noon meal. Christy was sitting on the schoolhouse steps, grading the children's arithmetic tests from that morning.

She set the tests aside, watching as Jared Collins and three of his men approached on horseback. They pulled to a halt just inches from the steps.

"Afternoon, Miss Huddleston," Mr. Collins said, giving her a tip of his hat.

"Sheriff Bell, Mr. Collins, Mr. Wynne." Christy nodded curtly. "Is there something I can do for you?"

"Let's not play games, Miss Huddleston." Mr. Collins dismounted. "There are plenty of rumors floating around that Prince returned here. The only question is where you people are hiding him."

Christy cast a glance at the children, who were listening solemnly. "I honestly do not know where Prince is," she replied. "But if I did, I wouldn't want to return him to your men. Not after the way we saw him treated."

Mr. Collins tapped his riding crop in his palm, his dark eyes gleaming menacingly. "If you *did* know, then you would be in possession of stolen property. That's why I've brought along the sheriff today." Mr. Collins lowered his voice to a whisper that only Christy could hear. "And my guess is he'll pay a lot more attention to a wealthy landowner like me than to a poor mission worker like you."

Nearby, the children were murmuring amongst themselves. "I'm sorry I can't help you," Christy said firmly.

"I'd really hate to see anyone in this little backwater place have to go to jail," Mr. Collins continued. "What would these poor, unfortunate children do with their teacher locked up?" He clucked his tongue. "That would hardly be setting a good example, now, would it?" The sheriff, a lanky man with a serious air about him, cleared his throat.

"I'm afraid Mr. Collins here has a mighty good point, Miss Huddleston. I can't overlook the crime o' horse-stealin'. Around these parts that's a mighty serious offense." Christy gulped. Suddenly the gravity of what was happening hit her. But what could she do?

After a moment, Ruby Mae stepped forward. "S'posin'—now, I'm just s'posin', mind you—that a body did know where Prince was? Would there be any kind o' reward for his capture?"

Mr. Collins grinned. "Why, of course, young lady. How about . . . hmm . . . how about a nice gold coin for your trouble?"

"Truth to tell, I had somethin' else in mind."

Uriah nudged Mr. Collins. "*Told* ya they know where he is."

"I'm not sayin' I know, and I'm not sayin' I don't know," Ruby Mae said casually. "I'm just sayin' what if."

"What is it you'd like for a reward?" Mr. Collins asked. "Just name your price."

Ruby Mae smiled, just a little. "I want a competition."

"A—a competition? I'm afraid I don't know what you mean."

"I mean a fair-and-square, you-and-me competition."

Uriah laughed loudly. "How about it, Mr. C? Maybe you could arm-wrestle her!"

Mr. Collins was not amused. "You're wasting

my time," he snapped at Ruby Mae. "Two gold coins. That's my final offer."

"You and me, ridin' to see who gets Prince. If'n I wins, the mission gets to buy back Prince. May the best man—or gal—win," Ruby Mae responded. She crossed her arms over her chest and gave Mr. Collins her most determined look. "And that's *my* final offer."

"B—but—" Mr. Collins spluttered. He turned to Christy. "Can't you do something with this urchin? She's obviously in possession of my property. Tell her to hand over the horse, or I'll have her arrested."

"To begin with, Mr. Collins, I think that's exactly what Ruby Mae is proposing." Christy winked at Ruby Mae. "You know, Ruby Mae," she said, "if I didn't know better, I'd say this accomplished equestrian is afraid to compete against you."

"Yellow-belly," one of the older boys muttered.

Lundy made a noise like a squawking chicken, and soon the other children were chiming in until the schoolyard sounded more like a barnyard.

"That's enough, children," Christy said, trying to quiet her students.

"You wouldn't want to embarrass yourself in front of your own employees, now, would you, Mr. Collins?" Christy asked sweetly. "I'm sure you can beat Ruby Mae in a simple competition. What do you think, Ruby Mae? Three clean jumps over the fence in the pasture?"

"Bareback," Ruby Mae added.

Mr. Collins cleared his throat. "What on earth is the point in this? He's my horse, you fools!"

"Ain't no point in ownin' him, if'n you can't ride him," Ruby Mae pointed out.

"Aw, go ahead, Mr. C," Uriah said, with a wink at his fellow stable hands. "She's just a mite of a girl. If you can't handle that stallion, ain't no way she can."

Mr. Collins gazed at the sky and let out a frustrated groan. "Oh, all right. We'll let the country bumpkins have their fun." He shook his riding crop at Ruby Mae. "But we'll do it on my terms. You have the most clean jumps over that fence, little lady, I'll let you have the right to buy back Prince for the same money I paid for him. I'll give you three months to raise the cash. You lose, he's mine, and you never go near him again."

"Mr. Collins, we can't possibly raise that kind of money!" Christy protested.

Mr. Collins shrugged. "I'm giving you the chance to get your stallion back. Take my offer, or I'll have the sheriff arrest you."

"It's all right, Miz Christy," Ruby Mae said nervously. "It's the best we can do."

"At least give us this much," Christy pleaded.

"If Ruby Mae wins, we get three months to come up with the money. During that time, Prince stays here at the mission, not at your farm."

"Fine. Whatever," Mr. Collins said with a dismissive wave. "One way or another, he'll be mine, soon enough."

Ruby Mae held out her hand to Mr. Collins, and after a moment, he shook it. "Wait here. Lundy and me'll go get Prince. In the meantime, you might want to practice up. Oh, one other thing. When we get him back, we want Prince's bridle and his blanket back, too."

"I don't know what you're talking about," Mr. Collins snapped.

"I'll take care of that matter, Ruby Mae," Christy said.

Ruby Mae nodded. "Then it's settled."

Christy followed Ruby Mae to a spot out of Mr. Collins' earshot. "Are you sure you want to do this?" she asked.

"He was goin' to find him eventually," Ruby Mae said with a sigh. "It was just a matter of time. We all knew it."

"But even if you win, you have to understand that we won't have the money to buy Prince back, at least not right now."

"At least we'll have the *hope* o' buyin' him. That's somethin'. Thanks to you."

"To me?"

"For givin' me this idea. Last night, you

were talkin' about how even powerful people like Mr. Collins have their weaknesses. So I got to thinkin' what his were." She chuckled. "And I said to myself, 'I can ride Prince and he can't.' And that's how I come up with the idea."

"You do realize we'll have to come up with some kind of punishment for your horse-napping," Christy said with a tolerant smile.

Ruby Mae considered this for a moment. "You know what, Miz Christy?" she said. "Even if'n you punished me with a hundred spellin' tests, it'd be worth it, if it meant I got to protect Prince from gettin' hurt."

Lundy joined them. "Guess we'd best be gettin' on," he said.

"So where has Prince been all this time?" Christy asked.

"Over to Lundy's," Ruby Mae said. "Safe and sound."

"I guarded him best I could," Lundy said.

Christy patted Lundy on the back. "Prince is lucky to have such good friends."

"Don't speak too soon, Miz Christy," Ruby Mae warned. "This ain't over yet."

❧ Seventeen ❧

An hour later, everyone assembled in the pasture to watch the great competition unfold. Miss Alice, Miss Ida, and David were there, and so was Doctor MacNeill, who'd run into Lundy and Ruby Mae as they were bringing Prince back to the mission.

Prince seemed happy to see all his old friends, and to be the center of attention once again. But as soon as he caught sight of Mr. Collins, he tried to bolt.

"Whoa, boy," Ruby Mae said soothingly, clinging to the horse's bridle. "He ain't a-goin' to hurt you. Not while we're around to protect you."

"I told you that horse lacks manners," Mr. Collins said. "You can't handle him any better than I can."

"Just keep your distance," Ruby Mae snapped, "and I'll handle him just fine."

"All right," Christy announced, "it's time for the competition to begin. Each participant will attempt to make three clean jumps over that fence. The person with the most clean jumps wins."

"And no saddle, neither," Ruby Mae reminded her.

"All jumps will be bareback," Christy added. "Now, who would like to go first? Why don't we toss a coin? Doctor MacNeill, you may do the honors."

Doctor MacNeill retrieved a coin from his pocket. "Ruby Mae, call it when I toss the coin in the air."

"Heads!" Ruby Mae called as the coin spun around.

"Heads, it is," Doctor MacNeill reported.

"Then I'll go first," Ruby Mae said.

While David helped Ruby Mae mount Prince, Lundy swaggered over to Mr. Collins. "She'll show ya how it's done," he said, hooking his thumb at Ruby Mae. "Even if she is a girl, she's the finest rider around these parts."

"I doubt that's saying much," Mr. Collins sneered.

Ruby Mae gave Prince a gentle nudge with her knees, and he took off at an easy trot around the pasture. They moved together effortlessly. When she eased Prince into a full gallop, it was breathtaking to watch. Horse and rider glided over the grass, Prince's hooves thundering on the ground.

"Look at 'em go," Mountie said to Christy. "Ain't it just the purtiest thing to watch?"

Ruby Mae moved Prince around until he was facing the broken piece of four-foot-high fence that the children used for practicing jumps. They approached at a nice, steady pace, never wavering.

At just the right moment, Ruby Mae eased forward, holding tightly to Prince's mane. In one graceful move, Prince launched into the air like a huge bird. He and Ruby Mae sailed over the fence, and for a moment, the sound of his hooves fell silent, and the only noise was the gasp of the crowd.

He landed gently just past the mud hole on the other side of the fence. Ruby Mae turned to the crowd and gave a confident wave. Her classmates roared their approval.

"Well, I'll be," Uriah muttered. "That gal can ride, all right!"

"Shut up, Wynne," Mr. Collins snapped, "or you'll be looking for work."

Twice more, Ruby Mae took Prince over the fence. Twice more, the crowd broke into happy applause.

Ruby Mae reined Prince in to an easy trot, and brought him back to Mr. Collins. "See?"

she said. "Ain't nothin' to it." She slipped off Prince and passed the reins to Mr. Collins. "Now let's see what you can do."

"Perhaps—" Mr. Collins gazed up at the stallion nervously, "perhaps we should wait a few minutes. After all, he's probably quite winded."

"Naw." Ruby Mae shook her head. "Prince could jump a dozen o' those without breakin' a sweat. He's all nice and warmed up for you. Go on. I can't wait to see how a real, for-true e-ques-tri-an rides."

❧ Eighteen ❧

Mr. Collins grimaced. "I'll need a leg up. Uriah, come here. Cup your hands, and I'll use them instead of stirrups."

Uriah obliged, groaning under the weight. Prince danced around nervously, but Ruby Mae held him steady.

Awkwardly, Mr. Collins settled on Prince's back. Ruby Mae stepped aside. "Good luck to ya. Remember, take it nice and easy."

"I don't need your advice."

Mr. Collins dug his boot heels into Prince's sides. The stallion reared up in surprise. Mr. Collins clung to Prince's neck, and after a moment, the horse settled down.

This time, Mr. Collins cracked his riding crop on Prince's flank, sending the horse into a wild gallop.

"Whoa, Nellie," Ruby Mae said, letting out a

low whistle. "That sure is some funny-lookin' ridin'!"

Struggling to control Prince, Mr. Collins took him around the field twice in an all-out gallop. Finally, with great effort, he managed to face the stallion dead-on toward the fence.

"He's goin' too fast," Ruby Mae whispered to Christy, as Prince pounded toward the fence. "Look—Mr. Collins is losin' his grip. See how he's a-startin' to slip off?"

Suddenly, just as they reached the fence, Prince changed his mind about jumping. He careened to one side of the fence, coming to an abrupt halt.

Whoosh! Mr. Collins did *not* stop. He flew through the air, right over the fence, and landed with a plop directly in the mud puddle on the other side.

After a moment, he let out a low moan.

"Mr. C!" Uriah called. "You all right?"

Doctor MacNeill, Christy, and the others all ran to check on Mr. Collins.

"You'd better let me check for any broken bones," the doctor said, kneeling beside the mud-soaked Mr. Collins.

"Unhand me!" Mr. Collins shook off the doctor and slowly stood.

"My, oh my. Would you look at those purty ridin' clothes, all a-covered with mud?" Ruby Mae said, barely concealing her smile.

"The . . . the brute!" Mr. Collins shook his

riding crop at Prince, who was nibbling on some grass nearby, not aware of the trouble he'd caused.

"If that's how an e-ques-tri-an rides, I think I'll stick to my way o' doin' things," Ruby Mae continued.

"Um, sir," Uriah said under his breath, "ya got mud on yer nose."

Mr. Collins pulled out a handkerchief and wiped his face, which only managed to make things worse. Several of the children began giggling uncontrollably. Even Uriah laughed.

"That—that four-legged devil isn't worth a dollar!" Mr. Collins cried to Christy. "You and your pathetic tots can have him!"

"You mean he's ours again, for good?" Ruby Mae cried.

"We'll pay you what you paid us for Prince," Christy said. "It may take us more than three months, but you'll get your money back."

"Just promise me I'll never have to see his ugly face again," said Mr. Collins, his voice almost a shout.

With that, he stomped off across the pasture.

Ruby Mae turned to Christy and hugged her. She ran to Prince and hugged him. She even ran to Lundy and hugged him.

"He's ours! He's really, truly ours!" she cried.

"Hooray for Ruby Mae!" Mountie exclaimed,

and soon the entire group was chanting the same thing, over and over again.

Ruby Mae hopped onto Prince and took a victory lap around the pasture, followed by her classmates.

"So the story has a happy ending, after all," Miss Alice said to Christy as they watched the joyful children.

"As always, Miss Alice," Christy replied, "you were right."

"I think this might be a good time for a prayer of thanksgiving, don't you?" said Miss Alice, and Christy couldn't have agreed more.

The next day, another letter arrived for Christy. She opened it to discover a copy of her newspaper article, sent by her mother. "You're the talk of the town!" she'd written at the top of the page.

After school, Christy held a ceremony in Prince's honor outside the school. First, she read the article about him aloud.

The children were ecstatic about being "famous"—so much so that they didn't even mind the punishment Christy imposed for their horse-napping escapade. For one month, they had to muck out Prince's stall, and feed and water him every day.

Prince, however, was completely un-impressed with his new fame. In fact, he tried to eat the article.

"Now that we're done reading—and nibbling—the article," Christy said, "I have one other thing I'd like to do. It's a presentation I've been meaning to make to Ruby Mae and Lundy."

Christy handed Lundy a wooden box. "Ruby Mae," she said, "why don't you open it?"

While Lundy held the box, Ruby Mae lifted the cover and gasped. "It's Prince's blanket! And his bridle! Miz Christy, how did you ever find them?"

"I've been saving them," Christy replied. "I had a feeling they might come in handy someday. That's one thing I've learned these past few weeks, children. Never, ever, give up hope."

Brotherly
Love

The Characters

CHRISTY RUDD HUDDLESTON, a nineteen-
   year-old schoolteacher in Cutter Gap.
GEORGE HUDDLESTON, Christy's fifteen-
   year-old brother.
MR. AND MRS. HUDDLESTON, Christy's parents.
AUNT LUCY, Christy's aunt.
**GRANDMOTHER AND GRANDFATHER
   HUDDLESTON**, Christy's grandparents.

CHRISTY'S STUDENTS:
   CREED ALLEN, age nine.
   LITTLE BURL ALLEN, age six.
   BESSIE COBURN, age twelve.
   RUBY MAE MORRISON, age thirteen.
   MOUNTIE O'TEALE, age ten.
   CLARA SPENCER, age twelve.
   JOHN WASHINGTON, age ten.

PRINCE, a black stallion.
GOLDIE, Miss Alice's palomino mare.

DAVID GRANTLAND, the young minister.

FAIRLIGHT SPENCER, a mountain woman who is a good friend of Christy's.

MR. BURNS, George's Latin teacher.

MISS MURKOFF, Mr. Koller's secretary.

PETER SMITHERS, a student at the Bristol Academy.

≫ One ≪

Miz Christy, I brung you some flowers. Some *magic* flowers."

Christy Huddleston smiled at nine-year-old Creed Allen, one of her most mischievous students. He stood before her desk, smiling his Tom Sawyer grin. His hands were empty.

"Invisible flowers," she exclaimed. "My favorite kind!" She made a show of accepting her imaginary bouquet. "Thank you, Creed. Now it's time to get to your seat. The noon break is over, and we've got an English lesson waiting."

"They ain't invisible, Miz Christy," Creed insisted. "They's *magic*."

He glanced over his shoulder at his classmates, who were watching him expectantly. Then, with a flourish, he waved his hand.

Suddenly, to Christy's amazement, he presented her with a bouquet of brightly colored paper flowers.

"Creed!" she cried. "They're beautiful! But . . . how did you ever—"

"Like I said," Creed said, strutting back to his desk, "they's magic."

Christy examined the colorful "bouquet." It was a simple magic trick. In fact, her own brother, George, used to perform the same trick when he was younger. But where on earth would a poor child like Creed get hold of something like this? Her students' families couldn't afford shoes or food, let alone magic paper flowers!

"You know, my little brother used to do a magic trick like this," Christy said.

"You mean George?" Creed asked.

"Why, yes. I guess I must have mentioned him before."

"No'm."

"Then how did you know his name?"

Creed grinned from ear to ear. "Could be 'cause he's hidin' behind that there blackboard, a-waitin' to surprise you!"

Before Christy could utter another word, out jumped George from behind the blackboard. He ran to her, lifted her right up out of her chair, and swung her around in a circle.

"Hey, there, Sis! Surprised?"

"George! I can't believe it's really you!" Christy laughed. "Now, please put me down. I'm getting dizzy."

George looked like their father, with his chiseled chin and his deep blue eyes framed by dark lashes. However, their faither had a solemn, worried air about him, but George always seemed ready to take on the world. And, like their mother, he had an infectious laugh and a dimpled grin that was hard to ignore.

Christy had also inherited their father's blue eyes, but she had their mother's delicate build. And when it came to personality, she was much more like their father than George was. She was responsible, kind, and quick to worry.

"Class," Christy said, straightening her dress, "I'd like you to meet my brother, George Huddleston."

"Oh, I've already met a few of these characters," George said, winking at Creed. "I taught Creed that magic trick during the break while you were reading to some of the other children. He's a quick study."

"How long have you been here?"

"Oh, just an hour or so. I walked from El Pano. Got lost a few hundred times. Then I did a quick tour of the mission. Love what you've done with the place, by the way."

"I don't understand," Christy said. "Shouldn't you be at boarding school?"

George rolled his eyes. "So much for the postal service. Didn't you get my letter?"

"Letter? No. I haven't had a letter from you in ages, George," Christy shook a finger at him, "even though I write you every single week."

"I know, I know—I'm the world's lousiest correspondent. But they keep us pretty busy at school, Sis. The thing is, I *did* write to tell you I was coming," he grinned, "Or warn you, I guess I should say."

"Don't be silly." Christy gave him a hug. "You know I'm thrilled to see you. But what about school?"

George picked up a piece of chalk from the blackboard. "We had a big storm the other day. It caused a lot of damage. The place is going to be closed for a couple of weeks while they do repairs."

"That's a shame."

"Well, it depends on your point of view. Most of us were pretty excited."

"Is it my turn?" Bessie asked as she gazed at George.

"Yes," said George rather matter-of-factly. "Introducing Bessie."

Bessie twirled in a circle and began pulling handkerchief's from George's coat sleeve. To the group's amusement, George acted more astonished with each handkerchief's appearance. As the laughter died down, George ran to the blackboard.

With a few quick strokes, George drew a

picture of Christy on the blackboard. In it, she was holding a paper flower in her teeth while she graded a stack of papers that towered to the ceiling.

The children laughed uproariously. Christy had to admit it was a very funny portrait. George had always been an excellent artist. In fact, he was good at almost anything he tried—when he applied himself.

"All right, class, settle down," Christy said, smiling in spite of her stern tone. "My brother is allowed to draw funny pictures of me, but I don't want the rest of you getting any ideas!"

"Well, well. Don't you sound just like a real teacher!" George exclaimed.

"I *am* a real teacher," Christy replied, trying not to sound defensive. She grabbed the eraser and removed the picture while the children groaned. "You know, I don't remember hearing anything about a bad storm around those parts," she said. "You'd think Mother might have mentioned it. I just got a letter from her yesterday."

George didn't answer. He turned to the class and said, "How about one more magic trick for the road?"

They applauded wildly. Christy sat at her desk and watched her crazy, wonderful, unpredictable brother "pull" a coin out of Mountie O'Teale's right ear.

Christy shook her head. Clearly, she had her work cut out for her. It was going to be very hard to top *that* performance with another grammar lesson.

≈ TWO ≈

My, my, will you look at that boy eat?" exclaimed Miss Ida at dinner that evening.

George ladled out another huge helping of mashed potatoes. "Finest food I've eaten in a long time, Miss Ida. You're the real magician around here."

Miss Ida smiled. "Your brother is such a charmer," she said to Christy.

Christy grinned with pride. Only a few hours had passed since George's arrival, and already everyone at the mission seemed to like her brother.

Miss Alice, who'd helped found the mission, had told Christy how bright and entertaining she found George. David Grantland, the mission's young minister, laughed uproariously at George's jokes. Miss Ida, David's sister, was clearly charmed.

And as for Ruby Mae Morrison, the thirteen-year-old girl who lived at the mission house—well, she was absolutely smitten. Christy could tell. She'd seen Ruby Mae and her friends go through all kinds of crushes at school. And if the doe-eyed look Ruby Mae was directing at George was any indication, Ruby Mae was already head-over-heels in love.

"Miss Ida, I ate up all your chicken, too," Ruby Mae said, grabbing for the last of the mashed potatoes. "How come you never compliment *my* eatin'?"

"Because you eat more than five full-grown men put together," Miss Ida scolded.

"Nonsense," Christy said, winking at Ruby Mae. "Ruby Mae has a normal, healthy appetite. Just like me."

George laughed. "It's true. Christy could out-eat me any day of the week." He shook his head. "I still cannot believe my big sister is a real, live teacher. To me, she's still just a kid with pigtails and dirty knees, playing with spiders."

"Spiders!" Miss Ida exclaimed.

"Oh, Christy always loved to learn about insects. It used to drive Mother crazy." George shrugged. "She always liked to find out where and how they live."

"So you're attending the Bristol Academy this year?" David asked. "Is that anywhere near Asheville?"

George finished off his glass of milk. "It's in Cullowhee, not too far from there."

"How do you like the school?" asked Miss Alice.

"I like it fine, although it's hard work, and the teachers are tough graders."

"Just like Miz Christy," Ruby Mae said softly. "I'll bet you're the smartest boy there, George."

"Hardly!" George scoffed.

"George doesn't always apply himself, Ruby Mae," Christy said, smiling at her brother. "If he did, there's no telling what he could accomplish."

"I don't always apply myself, neither," Ruby Mae admitted to George. "Applyin' makes my head spin."

"Ruby Mae, I think you and I are going to get along just fine," George said.

Ruby Mae gazed back at George like a lovesick puppy.

"So how long will you be able to stay, George?" David asked.

"A couple of weeks, at least. Maybe even longer. The fire did a lot of damage. Who knows?" George grinned at Christy. "Maybe I'll just stay here forever."

"Wait a minute," Christy said, frowning. "I—"

"All right, all right." George held up his hands. "I promise I won't stay forever, Sis."

"No, that's not what I meant. Did you just say *fire*? I thought you said the school was damaged by a big storm."

George paused to butter a roll before replying. "It was. But a fire started when one of the dormitory buildings was hit by lightning. That's where most of the damage was. Unfortunately, that's also where I was housed."

"What's your roommate doing while the repairs are being done?" Christy asked.

"Richard? I . . . I'm not sure. I think he decided to go home to Richmond. You know how he is. Very unpredictable."

"Well, all I know about him is what you mentioned in your letters. Which, I might add again, are far too infrequent. I hope you write Mother and Father more often."

"Not much," George admitted sheepishly. "Which reminds me . . . I didn't exactly tell them about my coming here."

"Why not?"

"You know how Mother is. I was afraid she'd be upset if she knew I was visiting you instead of going home." George met Christy's eyes. "So maybe we should keep this visit under our hats, if you know what I mean."

"Oh, I'm sure she'll understand, George. It's been ages since you and I have seen each other."

"Still," George said, a little more forcefully, "let's just keep it between you and me."

Christy hesitated. It didn't seem right, not mentioning something this exciting to her parents. She always told them everything in her letters.

"It's not like you'd be lying, Sis. We'd just be omitting a little information to spare someone's feelings." George turned to David. "What do you think, Reverend? You're an expert on such things."

"No, no." David shoved back his chair. "I'm off duty, George. And I don't want to get in the middle of a family dispute."

"I have an idea." George snapped his fingers. "I'll stop by Mother and Father's for a few days before it's time to go back to school. It'll be a complete surprise. In the meantime, not a word to them, Christy."

"All right. I hate to have you leave even a few days early, but Mother and Father will be thrilled to see you."

George gathered up some glasses and silverware. "I'll take care of the dishes tonight, Miss Ida. You've done enough." He motioned to Ruby Mae. "Come on, Ruby Mae. Give me a hand, and I'll tell you all about what Christy was like as a little girl. Did you know she sucked her thumb till she was ten?"

"Go on!" Ruby Mae cried.

"George Huddleston," Christy chided. "Don't you start—"

"All right, all right." George paused at the kitchen door. "I'm exaggerating slightly. But she did sleep with her stuffed bear, Mr. Buttons, right up until she left for Cutter Gap."

Miss Alice chuckled. "He's wonderful, Christy."

"An angel," Miss Ida said, "an absolute angel."

Christy laughed. "Well, I'm not sure I'd go that far."

She watched as George and Ruby Mae headed into the kitchen. George might not be an angel, but he was a wonderful brother. It would be great to have him here for a while to catch up on old times.

Christy found herself stopping to think about George's behavior. Why did she have this uneasy feeling that there was something not quite right about this visit?

❧ Three ❧

Slowly, carefully, George unpacked his belongings. He almost wondered if he should bother. It wasn't like he'd be staying here long.

He sat on the edge of his bed. It was covered by a threadbare but clean quilt. A battered wooden dresser, a chair, and a washstand completed the furnishings in the simple room. Not for the first time, George wondered about his sister's choice to work at the mission.

How different this was from the home they'd grown up in! The Huddlestons weren't a rich family. But compared to this spare house, their home back in Asheville practically looked like a palace.

George unpacked his socks and hairbrush. Then he reached to the bottom of his suitcase and pulled out a framed photograph.

The picture had been taken when George was eight years old. In it, George, Christy, and their parents were posed together formally. Mr. Huddleston looked stiff and dour. Mrs. Huddleston was smiling radiantly. George, as usual, was mugging for the camera.

But it was Christy's smile that made George love this photo so much. She wasn't looking at the camera. Instead, she was looking at George with a patient, loving, big-sister smile. It seemed to say, "I'll always take care of you, even if you *are* a lot of trouble, little brother."

He was startled by a gentle knock on his door. "George? It's Christy. May I come in?"

"Sure."

Christy stepped inside. "I just wanted to see if there's anything else you need."

"Nope. I'm all set." George spread his arms wide. "All the comforts of home."

Christy gave a wry smile. "This probably makes your dormitory look like a fancy hotel."

"I've got a bed. That's all I really need." George closed his suitcase and set it aside. "Although I have to admit that I'm impressed you've stayed here this long, Christy. How long have you been teaching at the mission now?"

"Almost a year."

George whistled. "To tell you the truth, I

probably would've hightailed it out of here the first day. I don't think I could stand the hardship."

"Actually, the mission is luxurious."

"Luxurious?" George cried.

"Yes, compared to most of the cabins around here." Christy went to the window and sighed. "These beautiful mountains! You'd never believe they could hide such poverty, George. Most of my students have never even owned a pair of shoes."

"It must be hard."

"Yes. And yet they're so brave and full of joy."

George shook his head. "I meant hard for *you*. This isn't your life, Christy."

"It is now."

"I mean, this isn't the way you were raised. And some people might say this isn't even your problem."

"But it is." Christy smiled that sweet, reassuring smile of hers. "I *chose* to be here. And I'm glad I did." She laughed. "Don't get me wrong. I mean, I had plenty of doubts at first. I almost gave up more than once. But I'm so glad I had the strength, with God's help, to stay. These people have given me so much more than I've given them."

For a moment, George just stared at his sister. They'd grown up together. They had spent every Christmas and Easter and Fourth of July together. They had enjoyed long, lazy summer vacations together.

And yet, looking at her now, she seemed like a stranger. Not only did she look different—older, stronger, more mature—she *seemed* different.

"How did you know, Sis?" George asked softly. "How did you know you made the right choice coming here?"

"I gave it time. I listened to my heart. And I prayed." Christy paused. "Then one day I looked out the window at those beautiful mountains, and I just knew this was the place I belonged, and this was the work I was meant to do."

George placed his belongings in the top drawer of his dresser. "I wonder if I'll ever feel that way. I never seem to know what the right thing to do is."

"You're only fifteen, George. You're not supposed to have all the answers."

"Oh, and you have all the answers at nineteen?"

Christy laughed. "Hardly." She reached for George's photo and grinned. "I remember when we had this picture taken. You refused to sit still. And you kept making an awful face at the poor photographer."

"That was just my natural expression."

"I'm so glad you're here. I've missed you. You know what I was thinking about the other day? Remember how we used to go to the church conference at Montreat every summer?"

"I think that's where your fascination with bugs really started."

"Well, I may have loved insects, but I certainly hated the water. You, on the other hand, were part fish from the day you were born." Christy sat on the edge of George's bed. "Anyway, I remember the day you tried to coax me into jumping off the pier into the lake. I kept saying I knew I would drown. And you kept promising you'd catch me." She sighed. "Finally, I jumped in. That had to be the hardest leap of faith I've ever made in my life. Harder even than coming here to work at the mission."

George squeezed her hand. "I'll always be there to catch you, Sis." He grinned. "Although, to be fair, you do weigh a whole lot more now than you did back then."

Christy swatted his arm playfully, then headed to the door. "If there's anything you need, just yell."

George watched the door close. He sighed. He needed Christy's help right now, and yet he could not bring himself to ask for her help. Could he trust Christy to stand by him now, or was that asking too much? George had a secret that he could not bear to share—not even with his big sister.

George's secret required more courage

than he could muster up, at least for now. That was a leap of faith that would have to wait for another day.

❧ Four ❧

Ａnd then there was the time she drew freckles on her face with a pencil. Seems she thought they'd make her look more sophisticated!"

Christy put her hands on her hips and groaned. They were talking about her again! George and Doctor MacNeill had been sitting on the mission house porch for the last hour, chatting and laughing. Three days had passed since George's arrival. It seemed as if there was no one in Cutter Gap he hadn't charmed by now. "George," she chided, "are you telling more stories about me?"

"Oh, I've learned all kinds of fascinating things about your childhood, Christy." Doctor MacNeill took a puff on his pipe. "For example, I found it fascinating to discover that before you decided to become a teacher, you aspired to be a beekeeper."

"That lasted about a week," Christy said as she sat down next to George. She shot her brother her most withering glance, but he just grinned good-naturedly. "You know, I could be telling all kinds of stories about your childhood, too."

"We haven't just been talking about you," Doctor MacNeill said. "Your brother's been keeping me in stitches. He has quite a repertory of jokes. Why, I'd say he's ready for the stage."

"You two really seem to be enjoying each other's company," Christy said.

"The doctor invited me over for dinner," George said. "He tells me he's quite the cook."

"I wouldn't know," Christy said, with just a hint of resentment. "I haven't had the chance to sample much of Neil's cooking."

"That's not true!" Doctor MacNeill exclaimed. "How about that picnic I took you on? I made corn on the cob and ham biscuits."

"Yes, but it took you months to invite me. You've only known George an hour."

The doctor's dark eyes sparkled. "Well, you don't know magic tricks, Christy," he teased. "George does."

George stood and stretched. It still amazed Christy to see how much taller he'd grown since she had last seen him. He was practically a man now—though she still couldn't help feeling he was her "little" brother.

"Well," he said, "I think I'll take a walk down to David's bunkhouse. He said he could use some help rebuilding his fireplace. Besides—" he winked at Doctor MacNeill, "I'm sure you two would like some time alone."

"What have you been telling him?" Christy asked as George headed off.

"Nothing but the truth. He asked if we were involved."

"And you said . . ."

"I said I wasn't sure," the doctor squeezed Christy's hand, "but that I hoped so."

Christy felt a blush creep into her cheeks. "And what did George say to that?"

"He said he thought the reverend seemed interested in you, too. I told George he was an astute observer." The doctor paused to tamp down the tobacco in his pipe. "Then he said he thought David was a great fellow."

"And you said . . ."

"I said he wasn't as astute an observer as I'd thought."

"Neil!"

The doctor chuckled. "I'm just pulling your leg. You ought to be used to that, growing up with George."

"True enough."

"He's great, Christy. You're a lucky girl to have him for a brother."

"Well, not altogether lucky," Christy said,

staring off at the garden to avoid the doctor's gaze.

"Meaning what?"

"It's just that he's been a bit of a disrupting influence at school. He asked if he could sit in on my class for a while, and of course I said yes. But before I knew it, he was disrupting everything. He had half the students trying to pull things out of their neighbors' ears."

"Excuse me?"

"You know the old trick, where you pull a penny out from behind someone's ear? Well, George taught the children the trick during the noon recess yesterday, and of course, pandemonium broke loose. Creed pulled an acorn out of Little Burl's ear. Ruby Mae pulled a hair ribbon out of Bessie's ear. Wraight even pulled a field mouse out of Lundy's ear."

The doctor pretended to look worried. "Remind me to check the children's hearing next time I'm here."

"I know it sounds funny, Neil. But the children are so in love with George that they barely pay any attention to me anymore. He's like the Pied Piper."

"It's just the novelty of a new face, Christy. Besides, he's only going to be here a couple of weeks at the most. It's silly to get jealous."

"I'm not jealous!" Christy cried, but as soon as the words were out of her mouth, she realized they weren't true. "Well, maybe I'm a little jealous." She sighed. "The truth is, I suppose I've always been a little bit jealous of George. Everyone always falls in love with him instantly. It takes me longer to get to know people. I'm shy. I don't tell jokes well. I can never remember the punch lines. And George is so . . ." Christy threw up her hands. "I don't know. So easy to like."

The doctor leaned over and planted a soft kiss on her cheek. "You're pretty easy to like yourself."

"Thanks, Neil, but you're biased."

"Actually, I would think you'd be a tough act for George to follow. You were the first child. You always excelled in school. And now you're here, doing something brave and difficult."

"Hmm. I never thought of it that way."

"I got the impression that George really looks up to you, Christy."

"Did he . . ." Christy hesitated, "did he happen to say anything else?"

"About what?"

"Oh, I don't know," Christy said casually. "About school. Any troubles he might be having."

"No, not a thing. Why?"

She shrugged her shoulders. "Just a feeling. I can't really explain it. I just have a hunch George isn't telling me the whole truth about why he's here."

"The storm—"

"Yes, I know. Like I said, it's just a hunch. Call it woman's intuition."

"Maybe," the doctor said, "you're looking for a problem where none exists because you're feeling a little uncomfortable about having George here."

Christy shook her head. "It could be you're right. I'll think about it. In any case, that's quite enough about my problems for one day. How about we try tackling yours for a while?"

"Mine?"

"For instance, what do you plan to feed George and me for dinner when we visit?"

"I don't recall inviting you," the doctor said with a sly smile.

"But you were going to."

"And how can you be so sure of that?"

"It's just a hunch. Call it woman's intuition."

❧ Five ❧

Sit next to me this afternoon, George!"

"No, me!"

"No, *me*!"

Christy ran to the rescue and pulled George out of the knot of girls surrounding him. As was usual during the noon recess, he had been the center of attention.

"My brother and I need to talk, girls," Christy said. Her words were met with a chorus of groans.

"Thanks for the rescue," George said, wrapping his arm around Christy's shoulder as they strode toward the schoolhouse steps.

"Normally, the boys and girls don't even like to sit near each other," Christy pointed out. "Do you realize that half the girls in my class are madly in love with you?"

"Only half?" George joked.

"Seriously. You'd better watch your step,

or you'll have Ruby Mae and Bessie battling over you."

"Like the reverend and the doctor are battling over you?" George wiggled his eyebrows in a teasing way. "Shouldn't they be dueling at dawn any day now?"

"They've called a truce," Christy grinned, "at least temporarily."

Christy and George paused on the schoolhouse steps. Out on the lawn, the children were gathered in small groups, waiting for the afternoon classes to begin.

"Mother said the reverend asked you to marry him," George said.

"He did. But I wasn't ready for a commitment like that. And I have . . . feelings for Neil."

"I thought so. Well, if you want my two cents' worth, either one would make a fine brother-in-law."

"I'll keep that in mind."

"And in the meantime, if Ruby Mae and Bessie inquire about *my* availability," George said, "just tell them I'm not ready for a commitment like that, either."

Christy went to ring the bell that signaled the end of the break, but just then, she remembered something. "I almost forgot. Miss Alice gave me a letter this morning. Mr. Pentland, the mailman, delivered it to her cabin by mistake. It's for you." Christy reached into the pocket of her long skirt and passed the envelope to George.

He glanced at the envelope, scowled, and stuffed it into his own pocket.

"It's from Richard, isn't it?" Christy asked. "I'd have thought you'd be glad to hear from him."

"Naw," George shrugged, "now he'll expect a response. You know what a lousy letter-writer I am."

"I noticed that the return address was from your school," Christy said, "but I thought you said Richard was going home to Richmond while they did repairs. I mean, the dormitory can't be lived in, right?"

"Hey, I don't go around reading *your* mail, do I?" George snapped.

"I'm sorry. You're right. It's just that I happened to notice the return address."

Instantly, George's expression softened. "I'm sorry, Sis. I didn't mean to bite your head off. Richard probably sent the letter from the train station before he left for Richmond. That's why he used the school's address."

"Oh, of course. That makes sense."

"So, time to ring the bell?" George asked.

"Ring away."

While George rang for the children, Creed Allen and John Washington dashed over to Christy. "Miz Christy?" Creed asked. "Is we a-havin' story time today?"

"Yes, Creed," Christy nodded. "I wouldn't miss it for the world."

She loved telling the children stories as much as she knew they loved hearing them. Since the school was too poor to afford books, sometimes Christy told Bible stories. Sometimes she recounted Aesop's fables, or stories she remembered reading as a child. And sometimes she just made up tales out of her own head. "As a matter of fact," Christy said, "I have a wonderful story in mind—"

"We was wonderin' somethin', Teacher," John interrupted, "that is, if'n you don't mind. We was wonderin' if maybe George could do the storytellin' today."

Christy hesitated. "George?"

"He's a powerful fine storyteller, Teacher," Creed said excitedly. "Keeps you in stitches, he does."

"Well, I suppose," Christy said slowly, "if George wants to tell you a story, it would be all right."

"Hooray!" John cried.

Christy watched as the two boys sprinted inside. She'd never seen them so excited about story time. At this rate, George would be ready to replace her before the week was out.

She wondered if anybody would even notice she was gone.

~ ~ ~

After school, George walked down to the

little pond near the mission house. It took a while to lose his trail of fans—Ruby Mae, Bessie, and Clara. But finally he found a quiet spot where he could be alone.

George took out the letter from Richard and opened it. The pages shook in his trembling hand.

He was not going to read the note. What was the point? There was nothing Richard could say to change what had happened.

There was nothing anyone could say.

Another letter would be coming soon enough. George could imagine his mother's beautiful handwriting. He could almost read her impassioned words. He could almost see the blurred ink, stained by tears.

As soon as she found out what had happened, she would write Christy. It shouldn't be much longer. He'd have to be ready to leave by then.

Slowly, George crumpled the letter into a tight ball. He tossed it far, far out into the pond.

It took a few moments to sink, but when it finally disappeared beneath the calm gray-blue water, he felt relieved.

That part of George's life was over. He was never going back to school. He was never going home again.

As George pondered his situation, only one question remained: where *was* he going from here?

❧ Six ❧

That evening, Christy crawled into bed with her diary. She'd gone to bed early. George was still downstairs with Miss Ida, Miss Alice, and David. From time to time, their laughter drifted up the stairs. Each time she heard their voices, Christy cringed a little.

She got out her pen and thumbed through the well-worn pages of her diary. Soon she would need to get another one. This one was nearly full. Full of the daily events of her life here at the mission. Full of hopes and fears and tears and laughter.

She was proud of this diary and what it represented. It was the story of her biggest triumph—coming here to teach. It was about learning, and growing, and making dear friends.

Her life in Cutter Gap was precious to her. It was an adventure of her own choosing. Hers, and hers alone.

Was that why she was feeling resentful about George's presence here? Did she feel as if this were her territory—something she didn't want to share, not even with her own brother?

Christy opened her diary to a fresh page. After a moment, she began to write:

I suppose I need to accept that Neil was right—I am jealous of George. As embarrassed as I am to admit that, it's the truth.

I love my brother dearly. But around him, I always feel like the <u>little</u> sister. People are drawn to him. Even my students seem to prefer him to me.

I know I shouldn't feel this way. But when I was sitting there at school today, listening to the children giggle at George's silly version of "Jack and the Beanstalk," I felt the old green-eyed monster— jealousy—eating away at me, the same way it did when I was a little girl and George sometimes stole away my parents' attention.

On top of all this, I still have lingering doubts about the real reason George is here. Today, for example, he acted oddly when I asked him about a letter he'd received.

Maybe I'm imagining things. Could it be that Neil is right, and I'm just looking for problems that aren't there because I'm feeling resentful of George?

Neil invited George and me to dinner tomorrow night. I have to admit that for a moment, even that simple, kind gesture from Neil made me resent George.

Just then, the sound of loud laughter met Christy's ears. She sighed and set down her pen.

A phrase from the Bible flashed into her head: "Charity envieth not."

Yes, the doctor had been right. It was jealousy she was feeling, all right.

She certainly hoped there was a cure.

— — —

"And if'n I add four and eight, then I got me thirteen?" Creed asked Christy the next day.

"Close, Creed." Christy took a deep breath.

It was time for arithmetic lessons, and as usual, the children were struggling. Why was she having such a hard time teaching addition to these children?

She'd asked David, who helped with the arithmetic classes, for advice, but he'd just smiled and counseled, "Patience, Christy. That's the secret. You need a sense of humor, and the patience of Job."

But with seventy children to teach and virtually no supplies, sometimes patience was hard to come by. Christy gazed around the room. The children were laboring over their chalkboards, doing the addition problems she'd assigned—harder tasks for the older students, simple counting for the very youngest.

"Try again, Creed," Christy urged.

The boy looked dejected. "I could figger it, I reckon, if'n I just had more fingers."

George, who was sitting nearby, signaled Christy. "Why don't I give a whack at explaining things?"

Christy's first reaction was to be annoyed. After all, *she* was the one with the teaching experience. *She* was the one who'd studied to become a teacher. George was just a high school student—and, come to think of it, not exactly a genius at mathematics, either.

On the other hand, she had sixty-nine other students in need of her attention.

"All right," Christy agreed. "Creed, George is going to explain this addition problem to you. Is that all right with you?"

"Sure thing," Creed said excitedly, clearly relieved to be exchanging instructors.

"Just don't do the work for him," Christy cautioned.

George gave her a mock salute. "Aye aye, Captain."

For the next few minutes, Christy made her way around the classroom, correcting students and answering questions. In the corner, George and Creed were giggling away. It hardly sounded like George was teaching the boy anything.

Just then, Ben Pentland, the mailman, appeared in the doorway. "Howdy, Miz Christy," he said. "I got a letter for you. Been a busy week for mail at the mission. Looks like this one's from Asheville."

George looked over. "From Mother?" he called.

"Probably," Christy replied, "I'm about due for another one."

"You sure it's not for me?" George asked, sounding oddly strained.

"Nope. Says to 'Miss Christy Huddleston,' plain as day," Mr. Pentland said.

"Don't worry, George. I'll let you read it," Christy said. She shook her head. "You know, you'd get more mail if you wrote more letters."

"I suppose you have a point there," George said sullenly.

Christy thanked Mr. Pentland, then joined George and Creed.

"So, how are we coming here?"

Creed beamed up at her. "I think I got it whopped, Miz Christy. If'n I got me four magic rabbits and eight magic rabbits, and I put 'em all in a big ol' hat, well, then, I'll have me twelve magic rabbits."

"That's right, Creed!" Christy said.

"I'll have me a passel o' baby rabbits, too, sooner 'n you can blink an eye," Creed said. "That is, if magic rabbits are anything like the ones that live around these here parts."

Christy glanced at George. "Magic rabbits?"

"I thought it might make the problem more interesting. It's no fun adding apples or stones. But magic rabbits, now, *they're* interesting!"

"Well, I guess the important thing is that it worked," Christy said grudgingly. "Thanks, George."

"He's a fine teacher, Miz Christy," Creed said.

"Yes, I guess he is."

Christy started for her desk. For a moment, hot tears stung her eyes. She always tried to make her lessons as fun and interesting as possible, she told herself. Just because George had come up with an inventive approach didn't mean she wasn't a fine teacher.

And yet . . . once again, there it was—the green-eyed monster.

"Sis?" George was right behind her. "Everything all right?"

Christy forced a smile. "Just fine. I was thinking about . . . about monsters, actually."

"Hmm. They might work even better than the magic rabbits."

"Maybe so."

George pointed to the letter in the pocket of Christy's sweater. "I was wondering. You plan on reading that?"

"Eventually. I usually wait until evening to read my letters. I like to save them. It gives me something to look forward to."

George lunged toward Christy and grabbed the letter.

He raced around the room holding the letter high in the air, taunting her. A few of the children started to giggle.

Christy was irritated, but more than that she didn't like the serious look that filled George's eyes. She couldn't help feeling that this was not a joke.

"George," she yelled, "it's my letter!"

"Mine," he said as he bounced merrily about the room.

"George, give me the letter" she said firmly.

Reluctantly George stopped and handed her the letter.

She shrugged. "I know it sounds silly. But around here, a letter is a big event."

"I was just curious to see how Mother and Father are doing. Maybe I could read it now, but not tell you what it says—"

"No, George!" Christy cried. "It wouldn't be the same at all. Half the fun of getting a letter is opening the envelope. It's like a present. You can read it when I'm done."

George looked annoyed, but Christy didn't much care. He was already taking over her friends and her job. The least he could do was let her enjoy her precious letter.

He started to turn away, but Christy touched his arm. "Thanks," she said.

"For what?"

"For helping with Creed. Maybe you should consider going into teaching."

George gave a strange, faraway smile. "I have a pretty good feeling my future's not heading in that direction," he said darkly. And with that, he left.

❧ Seven ❧

You're awfully quiet," Christy said to George.

"I'm just concentrating on not falling off the side of this mountain," he replied.

It was late afternoon, and the two of them were heading for the doctor's cabin. Christy was riding Prince, the mission's black stallion. George was on Goldie, Miss Alice's palomino.

The path to the doctor's was narrow but well-worn. By now, Christy was used to the sheer drop-offs and craggy peaks. But she was being careful to keep the pace slow, for George's sake. He'd seemed preoccupied on the trip—no doubt because of the steep trail. In any case, there was no point in rushing. It was a beautiful afternoon, a time to savor the rustle of the birch and hemlock and the musical rush of the mountain brooks.

"The children missed you this afternoon," Christy said. "Where'd you go?"

"Oh, just wandering," George said softly. "Taking in the sights. Thinking deep thoughts." He paused as Goldie stepped gingerly over a fallen log. "I hope I wasn't out of line today."

"Out of line?"

"You know. Trying to teach Creed. It's not like I knew what I was doing. You're the teacher. I'm not."

Christy glanced over her shoulder and smiled at George. "Well, I have to admit I was a little miffed. I've had such a hard time getting through to Creed, and then you step in with your magic rabbits, and *presto*— Everything's fine."

"Beginner's luck. Believe me, Sis, you're a great teacher." He sighed. "I wish there were more teachers like you at the Bristol Academy. You treat the children like real people. Not just scores on a piece of paper."

"Aren't there any teachers you like?"

"Oh, some are all right. But the headmaster, Mr. Koller . . . he's the worst."

Christy was surprised at the bitterness in her brother's voice. "What do you mean?"

George hesitated. "Oh, don't listen to me. You know I love to complain. Hey, up ahead— is that the doctor's cabin?"

"I told you I'd get you there in one piece."

"Now, if you can just get me back to the mission intact."

As they tied up the horses, Doctor MacNeill came to the door. "Welcome!" he cried, waving the spoon he held in his right hand. "You're just in time to help."

As usual, his cabin was a mess. The kitchen table was covered with a hodgepodge of medical books and glass bottles filled with drugs. The bookcase was layered with dust. Still, the cabin was a comfortable place. The air was sweet with something Christy couldn't quite identify.

"Shall I take your sweater?" the doctor asked.

"Thanks," Christy said, "it's warm in here."

"I've been cooking all day. That smell," the doctor said proudly, "is my very own rendition of rabbit stew. I got the original recipe from Granny O'Teale."

"Granny?" Christy asked doubtfully. Granny O'Teale was known for her strange mountain potions and herbs. Who knew what her recipe for rabbit stew would taste like?

"Have you ever made this before?"

The doctor grinned. "Trust me. I'm a chef at heart," the doctor assured her.

Then turning his attention to her brother, he asked, "What about you, George? Ever done any cooking?"

"I used to lick the spoon when Mother made chocolate frosting."

Doctor MacNeill passed him a wooden spoon. "Let's put your talents to the test. Go ahead and stir up that pot, would you?"

"What about me?" Christy asked.

"You can clear off the table and set it," the doctor instructed, "if you're feeling brave."

While Christy and George went to work, the doctor began making biscuits. Doctor MacNeill and Christy chatted away, but George remained distant and preoccupied—nothing like his usual buoyant self.

"So, George," the doctor said, "I think you have the makings of a fine chef."

"Today I told him he should consider a teaching career," Christy added.

"What is it you want to do for a living someday?" the doctor asked George. "Have you given it any thought?"

George shrugged. "I'd like to work for a newspaper, I think. You know—dig up stories, write on deadline. Maybe in New York, some big city like that." He looked out the window at the setting sun. "You don't even really need an education for that, I expect."

"Of course you do!" Christy exclaimed. "I'm sure they prefer to hire someone who's been to college."

"I used to know a guy named Jack O'Dell who wrote for the *New York Times*," Doctor

MacNeill said. "His brother and I went to medical school together. Jack started out as a paperboy for the *Times*. Hung around the place so much they let him start writing obituaries. Before you know it, he had by-lines on the front page nearly every day."

George seemed to brighten. "That's what I'm saying. I could do the same thing, if I wanted to. Start at the bottom, work myself up the ladder."

"George," Christy asked, eyeing her brother, "you're not thinking of quitting school—"

"No, no. Of course not. Can't you just see Mother's face if I did something that stupid?"

"Not to mention Father's," Christy added.

"Anyway, if all else fails and I can't be a writer, I'll always have a promising career as a magician," George joked.

"Better that than a chef," the doctor said, grabbing the spoon from George as the stew threatened to boil over.

~ ~ ~

Before long, Christy and George were sitting down at the table while the doctor ladled out large portions of his stew into bowls. When he sat down, he asked George to give thanks.

"Well, what are you waiting for?" the doctor asked expectantly after the prayer. "Dig in!"

"Ladies first," George said with mock politeness then grinned at his sister.

"No, no," Christy replied. "I insist you have the honor, George. After all, you're our guest. And I'm anxious to see what you think of a real, live mountain recipe. Granny O'Teale is known for her, uh . . . original approach to dining."

The doctor scowled. He sat down and scooped up a heaping spoonful of stew from his own bowl.

"Mmm," he murmured as he swallowed down the stew. A look of pure delight crossed his face. "Ambrosia. A meal fit for a king, if I do say so myself."

George took a deep breath. He dipped his spoon timidly into the rich, strange-smelling broth. "Oh, well," he said. "What's the worst that could happen?"

"You could die a slow and agonizing death," Christy replied with a straight face. "Fortunately, there's a doctor on hand."

Together, Christy and George each took a tiny bite of stew. Their eyes met in surprise.

"It . . . it's actually good!" Christy cried.

"Wonderful," George agreed.

Doctor MacNeill leaned back in his chair, arms crossed over his chest. "Oh, ye of little faith," he chided. "And what exactly did you expect?"

Christy just smiled in reply. "Pass the salt," she said, winking at George.

"Don't worry about cleaning up, George," Doctor MacNeill said again. "I'll take care of things after you leave. Just sit out here on the porch with Christy and me. It's a beautiful night. The stars are putting on quite a show."

"Oh, I don't mind," George said as he headed back into the cabin. "It's the least I can do after such a gourmet feast."

"Was that a hint of sarcasm I heard?" the doctor inquired.

"Not a bit," George said. "I loved the stew. As a matter of fact, the rabbit I use in my magic tricks may not be long for this world!"

"George, would you mind getting my sweater?" Christy asked. "It's getting a little chilly out here."

"Not at all."

As George retrieved Christy's sweater, he pulled out the letter from their Mother that was in the pocket. Would he have time to read it? And what if Christy noticed it was missing?

What does it matter now? he silently asked himself. *Getting caught reading a letter is the least of my worries.*

He slipped the letter into his shirt pocket and returned to the porch. "Here you go."

"Thanks, George," Christy said as she put on the sweater. She smiled at the doctor. "He didn't used to be so well-behaved."

"It's just an act for the doc's benefit," George said. "Now, you two sit tight. I'll be out in a minute after I get everything cleaned up."

Back in the cabin, George made a show of clearing off the kitchen table. Out on the porch, Christy and the doctor were deep in conversation.

If he wanted to know what was in that note, now was his chance.

George placed the doctor's teakettle back on the fire. When it started to steam, he held the envelope over the hot mist, just long enough for the wax seal on the back to loosen. He slipped a knife under the seal and it opened without cracking.

Carefully, he removed the sheets inside. *My dearest Christy,* the letter began. *I'm afraid I have some terrible news.*

≫ Eight ≪

George took a deep breath. He glanced over his shoulder. Out on the porch, the doctor was whispering something in Christy's ear. He turned back to the letter and read on:

> We have just received very disturbing news from George's school. I will recount the story to you as briefly as I can, and then you will see why your father and I are worried so about your brother.
>
> It seems that recently a large sum of money was stolen from the headmaster's office. Two students saw George and his roommate, Richard, in the vicinity of the office the evening that the money disappeared. When confronted about this, George instantly confessed to stealing the money.
>
> As awful as that is, there is more.

The next morning, George was summoned to the headmaster's office. But instead of appearing, he simply vanished without a trace! His suitcase is gone, along with a few clothes and belongings. He has not been sighted since—and this was several days ago.

"George?" Christy called. "Are you ever coming out to join us?"

"In a minute. I'm almost done in here. You two just relax. I may be slow but I'm extremely thorough. It's been so long since I've cleaned up, I've almost forgotten how."

"All right. But we should be getting home before too much longer."

George turned to the next page. His mother's careful handwriting had grown more frantic. And some of the words were blurred, by tears no doubt:

In his letter, the headmaster expressed his sorrow and anger about this incident. He had intended to expel George. After all, in this situation, what choice did he really have? But he did say that although he had often found your brother to be "a tad exuberant," he would be sorely missed. He seemed genuinely shocked at this turn of events—no more so, of course, than are your father and I.

Dear, have you had any word at all from your brother? I know how much he looks up to you. Perhaps he's contacted you by now.

I've tried to call you at the mission, but the operator tells me the new phone line is down for repairs. So I am sending this letter off in the hopes that you will write or call with news.

As you can imagine, we are beside ourselves with worry. We've even tried contacting your Aunt Lucy and Grandmother and Grandfather Huddleston. We didn't want to worry them, so we tried to give them as few details as possible.

I lie awake nights wondering how this could possibly have happened, Christy. George is such a good boy. What would possess him to steal money? Could it have been a dare, or some kind of pressure from the other boys? Could he need money and have been afraid to ask us?

Somehow, I think not. I know George has been accused of theft, but somehow I can't believe he is actually guilty. I know my son. He may have high spirits, but he is

*honest. And if he didn't take the
money, he couldn't have had much
spending money. How far could he
have gotten? And what if he's dis-
traught?*

*Your father is deeply worried, but
as I do, he also believes in George.*

*I must end this now, as the post-
man will be coming soon. As soon as
you receive this, please call or write
us without delay.*

*Love,
Mother*

George wiped away a tear. Carefully, he re-
folded the letter and placed it in its envelope.

Again he held the wax seal over the doctor's
teakettle. It softened enough for him to reseal
the envelope, although the "H" imprint his
mother had made with her wax stamp was
gone. Hopefully, Christy wouldn't notice. And
if she did, what would it really matter?

As George finished cleaning up, he cemented
his plans. He would leave early in the morning
before anyone else was up. He had enough
money for a one-way ticket to New York City.
Of course, when he arrived, he'd be flat broke.

But he was a quick thinker. He'd get a job
selling papers, like that friend of the doctor's.
Or he'd perform magic tricks on the street

for spare change. He'd find a way to get by. He'd have to.

Now his main concern was how to sneak the letter back into Christy's pocket. He feared she would miss it soon. He considered a dozen different options before finally deciding the simplest solution could be the best.

George returned to the porch. "Hey, Sis," he said, "I found this on the floor. Must've dropped out when I got your sweater."

"Mother's letter! I completely forgot about it. I'm glad you found it. I'd have had to ride all the way back here to retrieve it."

"I would have brought it to you," the doctor said. "It would have provided an excellent excuse to see you."

"Neil, you know you don't need an excuse to visit."

"I'm happy to report that I've also finished cleaning up," George interrupted. "At least, as clean as I'm capable of making it, which is probably not saying much. Thanks, Doc, for a great meal." He made a show of yawning.

"We really should be going." Christy stood. "It's a long way back, and it's slow going if we wait till it gets dark."

The doctor shook George's hand. "I'll be passing by the mission in a couple of days, George. You'll still be around, won't you?"

"I . . . yes, I suppose so."

"Well, I'll see you then."

"If I don't see you for some reason," George said, "I just want to say . . . well, I just want to say I think you and Christy make a great pair."

"As it happens, so do I," said the doctor. He gave Christy a gentle kiss on her forehead. "And thanks for the vote of confidence. But I'm sure I'll see you. Maybe you can even teach me one of those magic tricks of yours."

"Maybe so," George said softly. *But don't count on it*, he added silently in his thoughts.

I'm heading straight to bed," Christy said as she and George entered the mission house.

"Me, too. It's been a long day."

At the top of the stairs, George paused. "I just want you to know . . . well, I just want you to know that it's been great seeing you, Sis. I'm really proud of what you're doing here."

"That means a lot to me. I'm proud of you, too."

George scowled. "What have I ever done? Pulled a rabbit out of a hat? Told a few old jokes? You're doing important work here. You were wrong when you said I had the makings of a teacher today."

"But you do." Christy hesitated. "The truth is, I think the children would prefer you to me, given the choice. I have to admit, I've been a little jealous."

"Jealous? Of me?" George scoffed. "That's a laugh. Besides, teaching isn't about being entertaining for an afternoon. It's about having patience, day after day after day. And it's about trusting your students . . ." George's voice seemed to catch, "about having faith in them. That's what you do that's so important."

"Thanks, George." Christy gave her brother a long hug. "But this doesn't mean you're getting out of helping with the children's arithmetic class tomorrow."

"'Night, Sis."

"Goodnight."

Christy closed her bedroom door. She felt better, having admitted her feelings to George. And he'd said just the right things to help.

He really was getting more mature, she reflected. He was turning into quite a wonderful young man.

She took off her sweater and noticed the letter from her mother. She was so tired. Maybe she should save the letter for tomorrow, when she could enjoy it. Perhaps she'd read it out loud to George at breakfast.

In the meantime, her bed was looking extremely inviting.

It only took a few minutes for George to pack his bag—after all, there wasn't much to pack. He was relieved when he found some paper and a pencil in the top drawer of his dresser. But when he started to write a note to Christy, he realized he had absolutely no idea what to say.

What could he possibly write? That he was sorry? That he hoped Christy would understand he was really a good person, despite everything? That he hoped she and his parents would someday find it in their hearts to forgive him?

It all sounded so lame when he considered the torment of his mother's letter—the tears, the heartbreak. Were there any words in the English language to make pain like that go away?

George chewed on the end of the pencil. He could almost hear his English teacher, Mr. Drake, chiding him for the hundredth time, "Pencils are for writing one's most profound thoughts, Master Huddleston. They are not food for human consumption."

Old Mr. Drake. George would never see him again.

Now that he was leaving school behind for good, George had begun to realize just how much he'd enjoyed it. He might not have been the best student, but he liked learning. He liked his friends. In his own way, he even liked old Mr. Drake.

The blank page stared up at him. What could he write?

Well, at least he could try to write the truth:

Dear Christy:
All I can say is that I love you.
And that I'm sorry.

George

It wasn't the best letter in the world. But it was the best he could do.

— — —

He tried to sleep, but of course, he couldn't. He was dressed and ready to leave by the time the first pale pink tendrils of dawn made their appearance.

Carrying his suitcase, George slipped into the hallway and tiptoed down the stairs. Halfway down, he thought he heard someone in the hallway.

He paused, holding his breath. Nothing.

George ran the rest of the way down the stairs. He'd just grabbed the front door handle when he heard a voice.

"George? Where are you a-runnin' off to?"

George spun around. There stood Ruby Mae in the pale light. She was wearing a threadbare robe and an exasperated expression on her face.

"Ruby Mae! What on earth are you doing up at this hour?"

"I heard you a-sneakin' around." She crossed her arms over her chest. "So, where are you goin'?"

"Me? I'm not going anywhere."

"You're not goin' anywhere with your suitcase? Looks mighty strange to me."

"This? Oh, this just . . . uh, this has my magic tricks in it. Christy asked me if I'd do a little demonstration at school today. I was just taking my things over to get it all set up."

"You're a-goin' to do more magic for us?"

"Yep," George replied. Seeing Ruby Mae's thrilled expression, he couldn't help but feel guilty. But he was in this deep. And he had to escape without her waking Christy.

"I'll come with you," Ruby Mae said.

"Oh, no. You can't do that."

"But why? I could be your . . . what's that word? Your assister?"

"Assistant. That would be great. But I can't have anyone actually see how I set up my tricks. Then it wouldn't be magic anymore, don't you see?"

"You showed Creed how to make paper flowers. And you done showed everyone how to pull things outa ears."

"But a magician can't give away all his tricks. What fun would that be?"

Ruby Mae grimaced. "Can I at least be your assistant today at school?"

"I'd be delighted," George said. "Now, you go back to sleep. I'll see you soon."

He watched as Ruby Mae, grinning happily at her new assistant assignment, rushed back up the stairs. Quietly, George closed the front door behind him.

He hated lying like this. He hated leaving like this.

He'd thought he couldn't feel any worse about himself. But he was wrong.

✎ Ten ✎

I get to be George's assistant today," Ruby Mae announced when Christy came downstairs that morning.

Christy joined Ruby Mae, Miss Ida, and Miss Alice at the dining room table. "His assistant?" she repeated as she ladled oatmeal into a bowl.

"For when he does the magic tricks."

Christy frowned. "I'm afraid I don't know what you're talking about, Ruby Mae. Where is George, anyway? Is he up yet?"

"He was up at the crack o' dawn," Ruby Mae said. "I guess he had a lot of gettin' ready to do for the magic show."

"You saw him this morning?"

"He was just headin' out the door with his suitcase. That's when he told me I could be his assistant. I hope I get to wear a costume."

Christy glanced at Miss Alice. "Did you say *suitcase?*"

"He puts all his tricks in there. He was takin' 'em over to the school."

"I think I'd better check on this." Christy pushed back her chair. She had an icy lump in the pit of her stomach. George had been so quiet yesterday evening. And now, here was this story about him sneaking out the door at dawn, carrying a suitcase. She had a bad feeling.

With Ruby Mae at her heels, Christy ran across the dewy yard to the schoolhouse. Nervously, she pushed open the door.

"B—but there ain't nobody here!" Ruby Mae cried.

Ruby Mae ran to the front of the room, checking everywhere for a sign of George or his magic tricks. But after a few minutes, she turned to Christy, defeated.

"I don't understand," she said.

"I'm afraid I don't, either, Ruby Mae," Christy said.

Back at the mission house, Christy and Ruby Mae hurriedly headed straight upstairs to George's room.

Christy knocked softly on his door. No answer. Slowly she opened it. His bed was neatly made. His dresser was empty.

"He left a note!" Ruby Mae exclaimed.

Christy read the simple letter. "What does

it mean?" she wondered aloud. "What is he sorry about?"

Ruby Mae scowled. "For runnin' off without even sayin' his goodbyes proper-like, I reckon. And to think I was hopin' to marry him someday! Your brother ain't the least bit reliable, Miz Christy. If'n you don't mind my sayin' so."

"George is a little unpredictable sometimes," Christy admitted, "but he's never done anything like this before."

They returned to the dining room. "So?" Miss Alice asked. "What's the verdict?"

"I don't know what a verdict is," Ruby Mae snapped, "but I'll tell you this much—there ain't goin' to be no magic show today. Not unless you count George disappearin'."

"He's gone," Miss Ida cried, "without saying goodbye?"

"It looks that way," Christy said. "He left me a note, but I don't really understand what it means," Christy passed the letter to Miss Alice.

"But George is such a polite boy—so charming." Miss Ida clucked her tongue. "This just doesn't seem like him."

"It isn't," Christy agreed. "That's why I'm worried."

Miss Alice stared at the note. "Was anything bothering George?" she asked. "Perhaps a problem at school? A girlfriend?"

"Girlfriend!" Ruby Mae cried. "George was sweet on somebody?"

"Not that I know of, Ruby Mae," Christy said.

Miss Alice patted Christy's arm. "I'm sure there's a logical explanation, dear. He's probably heading back to the station at El Pano. Why don't you take Prince and go look for him?"

"But what about school?"

"David and I will take care of teaching today. You'll do everyone a lot more good by getting to the bottom of this mystery."

Christy gave her a hug. "Thank you, Miss Alice. I'm just going to run upstairs and get my sweater, and I'll be on my way."

"I'll fix you up a sandwich for the road," Miss Ida volunteered.

"Thanks, Miss Ida. That would be great." Christy hesitated. "Would you mind making two? Just in case I can talk George into coming back?"

"Of course. You just tell that boy we expect him at dinner this evening, promptly at six."

"And tell him his assistant is mad as a wildcat that he up and left without doin' a magic show," Ruby Mae added.

Christy managed a smile. "I will, Ruby Mae."

She ran upstairs, two steps at a time. There

had to be a logical explanation. There just *had* to be.

Christy donned her sweater. She was starting down the stairs when she felt the envelope from her mother in her pocket. She pulled out the letter and returned it to her dresser. She didn't want to risk losing it on her ride.

As she set it down, she noticed something strange about the wax seal on the back. Her mother's usual initial imprint was gone, as if it had melted. And the wax was barely sticking to the envelope.

Suddenly, she pictured George, bringing her the letter at the doctor's cabin last night.

Something was very wrong here.

Christy slipped her finger under the seal and pulled out her mother's letter.

My dearest Christy, she read. *I'm afraid I have some terrible news.*

Her heart in her throat, Christy read on. When she was done, she wiped away a tear.

Now at least, George's recent actions made more sense to her. He had come to Cutter Gap to hide from their parents and the school's headmaster.

Christy began to examine her beliefs about her brother. *It isn't like George to steal, but it also isn't like him to read other people's mail,* she thought.

Christy wasn't sure whether to be angry at George or to be compassionate about his situation. Either way, she knew only part of the reason for George's sudden disappearance, and she knew she was going to find him to hear his side of the story. *George may not know it,* she thought, *but he needs his big sister right now.*

❧ Eleven ❧

W̲ell, I have to admit it doesn't look good," David said as he helped Christy saddle up Prince.

She'd shown David her mother's letter. He'd read it twice before reacting.

"I keep thinking there must be more to the story," Christy said, but she could hear the desperation in her own voice. "Hoping, anyway."

David spread a blanket over Prince's broad back. "The thing is, he ran away, Christy. If he didn't take the money, why would George have run?"

"I've asked myself that, too. And I don't have an answer." Christy rubbed her eyes. She was already tired, and the day had just begun. "But why would George steal money, David? Father sends him an allowance. George has always had everything he needed."

David shrugged. "Who knows? Maybe he had a girlfriend he wanted to impress. Maybe he owed someone money and couldn't pay it all back. There could be a hundred reasons. In the end, it doesn't really matter what his reason was. What matters is that he did something wrong, and now he has to face up to the consequences like a man."

"He's a good person, David. A little impetuous, to be sure. But I know he has a good heart."

David positioned Prince's saddle. "Why don't I ride with you, Christy? You're in no mood to be alone right now. And Miss Alice can handle school today."

"No. You have plenty of other work to do."

"You don't even know what direction he headed."

"It's a pretty safe guess he's going back toward El Pano. At least, that's as good a place to start as any. And in any case, George is my brother. This is my problem."

David patted her shoulder. "The truth is, it's George's problem, Christy. He's the one who made the mistake. And only he can correct it."

"First of all, I believe in my brother. He would not steal. And think how alone he must feel right now. He's afraid to go home. He's afraid to go back to school. And he's afraid to come back here." Tears burned her eyes. "I know things don't look good for George right now. That's why he *needs* a friend more than ever. He needs me."

———

How could the morning be so beautiful, Christy wondered, when she felt so gloomy?

The trail to El Pano snaked through the mountains past rocky chasms and sheer cliffs. Swift-moving streams followed much of the route. The thin path was covered with a thick canopy of trees. Patches of sunlight dappled the forest floor.

Christy tried to occupy herself with other thoughts. For a while, she identified wildflowers that her friend, Fairlight Spencer, had shown her.

But always her thoughts strayed back to George. And always the questions remained. Why had he done such a thing? And why had he run away—from school, and then from her?

Minutes passed, slowly turning into hours. The sun was high in the sky now. After a while, Christy found a shady spot by a pair of birch trees. She stopped there and decided to eat the sandwich Miss Ida had prepared. But as soon as she unwrapped the sandwich, she realized she wasn't the least bit hungry.

Something was wrong. She should have

passed George by now. Even giving him a good head start, she had the advantage of a swift horse. For someone walking with a suitcase, this would be a tedious and tiring route.

Perhaps she'd been wrong to think George would come this way. How did she know what he was thinking? After all, she would never have dreamed he would get himself into this kind of trouble. Who knew where he was heading next?

With a sigh, Christy wrapped up her uneaten sandwich after giving the vegetables to Prince. She wondered how much farther she should travel. If she went all the way to El Pano, she'd never get back to the mission today.

Another hour, she promised herself. Another hour, and then she would give up.

"Christy."

The voice came from behind her on the path. For a moment, Christy froze. She thought it sounded like him, but sound in these woods could be distorted. And there were plenty of unsavory types lurking in the forest.

Slowly, she turned her head.

As if by magic, George stepped out of the woods.

"Hey, Sis," he said softly.

"But . . . how could I have missed you? Did I ride right past you?"

George gave a sheepish grin. "I heard you

coming and I hid in some bushes. Then I started having second thoughts."

Christy stared at her brother. He was in the middle of the path, his suitcase tightly clutched in his right hand. Standing here in the middle of this vast forest, he looked surprisingly small, like a little boy. His hair was mussed. He had a scratch on one cheek. His clothes were wrinkled.

He looked so vulnerable—not at all like the cocky, self-confident George of a few days ago. He looked lost.

He looked like someone who needed a big sister.

Christy walked to his side. She put her arms around his shoulders and pulled him close. He stiffened, then relented. With a sigh, he rested his head on her shoulder.

"Oh, Sis," he whispered, "I've really made a mess of things, haven't I?"

"Maybe I can help," Christy whispered, "if you let me."

"Nobody can help. It's too late."

"It's never too late. Not if you pray for God to guide you through this."

George looked at her pleadingly. The desperation in his eyes was almost more than she could bear.

"George," Christy said sternly, "It's time for the lying to stop. Why are you *really* here in Cutter Gap?"

❧ Twelve ❧

George stared at his sister, searching his heart for the right answer. At last he said softly, "Didn't you read Mother's letter?"

"Yes. But it just made me think of a hundred questions to ask, George. It didn't give me any answers. Only you can do that."

And I'm not going to, George thought. *Not ever. I'm a man of my word, and my lips are sealed.*

"Let's start at the beginning," Christy said, using the same tone of voice she reserved for her most difficult students. "The money. Did you take the money, George?"

George kicked at a loose stone in the path. "Mother and Father seem to think I did. Don't you?"

"I don't know what to think. But I do know that you're a decent, honorable person."

"Well, even decent, honorable people make mistakes."

"But why?" Christy's blue eyes were clouded with confusion. "Why would you take money from the headmaster's office and risk everything? It just doesn't make any sense."

"Why does it matter now, Sis? What's done is done. I'm out of the academy. I can't go home."

"You can always go home, George. Mother and Father will always stand by you. And so will I."

"I don't need anyone. I'm going to New York City to become a writer."

George almost laughed at how ridiculous he sounded. He was surprised and touched when Christy didn't even smile.

"You'll make a wonderful writer someday, George. Or artist. Or—" Christy smiled, "magician. I think you can do anything you set your mind to. But you need to finish your education first."

"Well, I don't think the Bristol Academy will be welcoming me back with open arms. But sure, I'll try to go back to school someday." George threw back his shoulders and did his best to project a confident smile. "Well, I'd better be on my way. It's a long walk to El Pano."

Christy grabbed his arm. "George, whatever happened back at school, you have to

face it. You can't run from your problems.
They have a way of following you."

"Like my big sister?" George tried to joke.

"I can help you. I know I can, if you'll just
let me."

George shook off her hand. "Christy, I'm a
big boy. I can handle my own problems."

"At least let me give you a ride to El Pano.
It's a long trip on foot."

"No."

Christy's face froze into a grimace of frus-
tration. "You can be so pig-headed and
stubborn and unreasonable!" she cried.
"Sometimes I feel just like I did when you
were a little boy. Mother would ask me to
call you in for dinner, but you'd be busy
playing and you'd ignore me, no matter
how I pleaded."

"What can I say?" George forced a grin.
"I'm your little brother. It's my job to torment
you."

Just then, George heard the sound of
voices, coming from beyond the next ridge.
A moment later, a tall, gaunt man George
recognized as Mr. Pentland appeared, carrying a small mail bag.

But it was the person walking beside him
who made George's heart do a somersault.

Richard!

What was his roommate doing here? Now?

Frantically, George's eyes darted about. His

first reaction was to dive for cover, but of course, that was ridiculous.

He was trapped.

"Well, well, who do we have here?" Mr. Pentland called. "Miz Christy, I declare. Ain't often I meet up with company on this here route. And George, too!" Mr. Pentland elbowed Richard. "Seems you found him sooner 'n you figgered."

Richard and George locked eyes. Richard was a small, slight boy, with curly blond hair and wide, hopeful eyes. He was dressed in his worn brown jacket and a too-large pair of pants that had once belonged to George. Richard's family didn't have much money, and George often lent him clothes.

"Richard," George said darkly, "I should never have told you I was coming here. Why are you here? There's no point." He paused, making his next words emphatic. "*Everything is decided.*"

Richard ignored George. He approached Christy and shook her hand. "You must be George's sister. I've heard so much about you, Miss Huddleston. I'm Richard Benton, George's roommate from the Bristol Academy."

"Richard!" Christy exclaimed. "Yes, George has spoken of you. But how . . . why are you here?"

"Good question," George muttered.

"Well, that's a long story." Richard paused. "How much does she know, George?"

"She knows all she needs to know," George said. "If you have something to talk about, Richard, let's do it privately."

"Didn't you get my letter?" Richard asked.

"Yes, I got it."

"Well, then—"

"I didn't read it, Richard. I threw it in a pond without even opening it."

Richard took a step closer to George. He had a fierceness in his eyes that George had never seen before. "Look, we can talk now, in front of Christy and Mr. Pentland, or we can talk later. But we're *going* to talk, George Huddleston."

George gazed up the path, then back. All he wanted to do was run. But he was trapped. He *had* to deal with Richard. And he didn't want Christy to get caught up in the middle of everything.

"Whatever it is you two have to discuss, why don't you do it back at the mission?" Christy interjected.

George sighed deeply. "All right. One more night, and then Richard and I leave in the morning. But there's one condition."

"What's that?" his sister asked.

"No questions. All right?"

"No conditions, George," Christy replied. "You're my brother and I love you. I want to help you. And if that means I have to ask some hard questions, so be it."

"All right, then." George gave her a stiff smile. "You can ask all the questions you want. But I'm not guaranteeing I'll answer any of them."

⫷ Thirteen ⫸

H e's back!" Ruby Mae cried. "George is back!"

As Christy, George, Richard, and Mr. Pentland approached the mission house, they were met with a flurry of activity. Ruby Mae ran to greet them, and Miss Ida, Miss Alice, David, and the doctor appeared on the porch.

"Neil!" Christy exclaimed. "What are you doing here?"

"Just stopped by to check on the reviews of my dinner," the doctor said, glancing over at George. "Actually, I was running low on some medical supplies, and thought I'd see if Miss Alice had any she could spare." He paused. "It seems you found your brother."

Everyone fell silent. All eyes were on George.

He stopped in his tracks at the foot of the porch steps. "Look, I know you all are wondering what's going on," he said softly, a pained expression on his face. "I . . . all I can say is that I'm sorry I left so abruptly, especially after all your wonderful hospitality. But I don't want to talk about this. It's private." He glanced sharply at Richard. "This is Richard, my roommate from school. He and I will be leaving in the morning. Come on, Richard."

The two boys headed into the house. Ruby Mae tugged on Christy's sleeve. "What's a-goin' on, Miz Christy? Nothin' George said makes a lick o' sense. What happened?"

"I don't know, Ruby Mae," Christy said in a determined voice. "But I'm about to find out right now."

~ ~ ~

"Go away."

Christy knocked on George's door again. "We need to talk, George. I still have some questions."

"And I didn't promise you any answers."

This time, Christy pounded on George's door. He wanted to be stubborn? Well, she could be just as stubborn . . . and then some!

"I'm not leaving this hallway, George."

A moment later, George's door opened a crack. "Christy, Father always said you were the most pig-headed girl he'd ever had the privilege of knowing."

"Well, Mother always said you're so stubborn you could be part mule!"

George stared at his sister through the crack. Christy could see the start of a smile on his face. "You're really not going to leave me alone, are you?"

"No, I'm not."

The door swung open. Richard was staring out the window. He nodded at Christy, then returned his gaze to the beautiful mountain vistas.

Christy sat down on George's bed. "All right. I'm listening."

"Just then, you sounded exactly like Father," George said quietly. "You're not my parent, you know."

"I'm your sister, George. I love you. I'll stand by you, if you will just help me understand what's going on."

George stared at his reflection in the small mirror mounted over his dresser. "I'm a man now, Christy. I have to take responsibility for my actions."

For the first time, Richard spoke up. "I believe I'm the one who's supposed to say that line."

"What do you mean, Richard?" Christy asked, surprised.

Richard turned to face Christy. He bit on his lower lip to keep from crying. "I'm the one who's not taking responsibility for his actions."

"Richard . . ." George said in a low, warning voice.

"I have to tell her, George. I have to clear my conscience."

"Don't be a fool! The damage is already done—"

"Miss Huddleston," Richard said in a choked voice, "George didn't take that money from the headmaster's office. I did."

❧ Fourteen ❧

You?" Christy exclaimed.

"Don't listen to him, Christy," George began, but Richard waved him aside.

"I'm ashamed to admit it, but yes, I'm the one," Richard said then lowered his head in shame. "I sneaked into the headmaster's office by picking the lock on his door." He shrugged. "It wasn't so hard, really."

"But I don't understand." Christy frowned. "Why did George say he took the money?"

"Because he was trying to be a good friend," Richard said. "He was wrong to cover for me that way, but he meant well." Richard slumped onto the bed next to Christy. "You see, George knew how short my family is for cash. I'm on a full scholarship at the academy." He smiled crookedly. "Even my clothes are hand-me-downs. George gave me this jacket and these pants."

"Richard," George said, his voice softened, "you don't have to tell my sister all this."

"But I *want* to, George, don't you understand? There's nothing worse than carrying around a terrible secret like this."

Christy touched Richard's shoulder. She was surprised that he was trembling. "Go on, Richard."

"Well, George figured if I were expelled for taking the money, I wouldn't ever be able to get into another school. Who's going to give a scholarship to someone who's been expelled for stealing?"

Christy looked at her brother sharply. "But doesn't the same logic apply to you?"

"Maybe." George gave one of his I-can-handle-anything smiles. "But I have a way of landing on my feet, Sis. And Richard—well, he's got a lot to deal with right now. His father worked for the railroads, but he hurt his back last year. Richard has three younger sisters, and the family's pretty hard-up for money."

Richard shook his head. "I should have quit school and gotten a job to help my family a long time ago. But my parents insisted that I finish school. They said that way I could get a good job later on, a real one." He paused, looking a little embarrassed. "I always thought I might become a doctor. You know—to help people like my father."

"I know how hard it must be for you and

your family, Richard," Christy said gently. "I've seen poverty here in Cutter Gap that I never even imagined could exist. But I'm sure you realize it doesn't justify taking money that doesn't belong to you."

Richard started to speak, but George stepped in. "Christy, Richard's little sister broke her leg a few months ago. They didn't have the money to have it set properly, and the leg didn't heal correctly. Now she's in constant pain, and the only thing that can help her is surgery."

"Surgery," Richard added, "that my father simply can't afford."

"Oh," Christy said. "I see."

"The doctors said if they had enough money for a first payment, they'd go ahead with the surgery." Richard wiped away a tear. "I thought . . . well, I know I was wrong, but I thought if I could help Abigail, it'd be worth any cost. I guess I didn't really think things through."

"I told you not to worry," George said brightly. "I've got everything under control."

"No, you don't, George. I should have listened to you that night," Richard said. He turned to Christy. "After I told George what I'd done, he tried to talk me into turning myself in. He said the headmaster would understand, and that I wouldn't be able to live with myself if I kept the money. But then the headmaster's assistant came to our dormitory door . . ."

"What did he say, Richard?"

"He said that somebody had seen George and me in the area that night. That's true, Miss Huddleston. I told him I wanted to take a walk, and he headed back to our room. But George didn't have any idea what I was planning. George is completely innocent. You have to believe me."

Christy glanced at her brother. "I do."

"And when George spoke up and said *he'd* taken the money, I just went numb," Richard continued. "After he left, I wrote him here, since he'd told me this was where he was heading first. I told him how badly I felt about everything."

"But what's done is done, Richard," George said. "I'm going off to New York City to seek my fame and fortune, and you, my friend, are going to go straight back to school. Someday, I'll be a famous writer and you'll be a famous doctor, and we'll get together over dinner and laugh about all this."

George's words hung in the air. Richard slowly shook his head. "No, George. That's not what's going to happen. What is going to happen is that I'm going to go back to school—with you—to tell everyone the truth."

"And what about Abigail?" George quickly shot back.

Richard didn't have an answer, but Christy did.

"If Abigail loves her brother as much as I love mine," she said, "then I don't think she'd want him to make this kind of sacrifice for her."

"There's no point in going back," George argued. "The headmaster won't let me off. He'll say that since I knew about Richard's crime, I should have turned him in right then and there instead of covering for him."

"But you tried to talk me into turning myself in!" Richard cried.

"It doesn't matter." George shook his head. "What point is there in both of us getting expelled? This way, at least you'll have a chance to finish school."

"I can't let you do that," Richard replied. "Besides the truth will come out anyway when I return the money."

"You have to tell the truth and clear the air, George," Christy said. "It's the only way. I'll go with you, if you like."

George hung his head. "This is all such a mess. I just wanted to help. . . ."

"Things might just work out better than you've imagined," Christy said. "You never know. I've seen some real miracles since moving here to Cutter Gap."

"I don't know, Sis. I think it's too late. I don't think I can go back there now. I couldn't face everyone after all the lies I told. Especially Mother and Father."

"Trust me, George. I'll help you get through this." She squeezed his hand. "Remember that leap into the water I took, back when we were children? Well, it's time for *your* leap of faith."

✎ Fifteen ✎

Personally, Christy," said Miss Ida, "I don't see why you're going to the academy with your brother. After what he did, perhaps he should face the music himself."

Dinner was over, and Richard and George were upstairs. By now, everyone knew the whole story, which Christy had explained. All through dinner, Richard and George had sat quietly, avoiding all eyes. The conversation had been polite, except for a few intrusive questions from Ruby Mae. Still, both boys had barely touched their food.

But now that Richard and George were safely out of earshot, everyone seemed to have an opinion to share with Christy.

"Seems to me when a young man lies to his own flesh and blood, the last thing he deserves is a second chance," Miss Ida said as she cleared the dining room table.

"But George meant well, Miss Ida," Christy argued. "I'm not defending the fact that he wasn't honest with us, but he did mean well."

Miss Ida clucked her tongue. "That boy deserves to be punished, if you ask me."

Christy went out onto the porch, where David, the doctor, and Miss Alice were sitting. "Miss Ida thinks I'm being too gentle with George," she told them. "How about the rest of you?"

"Well, as it happens, we were just discussing that very matter," said the doctor.

Christy leaned against the porch railing. The wind was gentle on her face, and sweet with pine. "And what was your conclusion?"

"In the end, the only thing that matters is *your* conclusion, Christy," said Miss Alice.

"I just keep thinking of Luke 6:31," Christy said softly. "'As ye would that men should do to you, do ye also to them likewise.' If I were in George's shoes, I would want him to stand by me at a time like this. After all, I'm his sister. I love him." She looked at Miss Alice. "Isn't that what it all comes down to?"

Miss Alice smiled her lovely, luminous smile. "I think you've already answered your own question."

~ ~ ~

The next day they reached El Pano after a long, tiring walk. After spending the night at a boarding house, Christy insisted that they stop at the general store first thing the next morning.

"Shouldn't we be going straight to the train station?" George asked, consulting his pocket watch.

"We have plenty of time," Christy said. "Not much money, but plenty of time."

"I promise I'm going to pay you and George back every cent you're lending me," Richard vowed.

"Don't you worry about it," Christy replied. "We're glad to help."

Richard wrung his hands together. "I already owe you and George so much. And Doctor MacNeill, too. Did I tell you he said he was going to make some inquiries about my sister's surgery? He said he had some doctor friends who might be able to help."

"He also said not to get your hopes up," George reminded him gently.

"Still, for him to even try . . . well, it's awfully nice of him."

"So," George said to Christy, "did you want to buy something here at the store?"

Christy pointed to the telephone in the corner of the cramped store.

"Not buy. Call. Miss Alice told me that the owner will let us use their telephone, since the one at the mission isn't working."

"A call?"

"To Mother and Father."

George took a step backward. "I can't do that, Christy."

"You have to. Mother and Father are worried sick about you."

"They're more angry than worried." George looked past her. "I . . . I'm not like you, Christy. You're the one they're always proud of. The one they can count on. Me, I'm just the family clown."

Christy couldn't help smiling. "You know what's ironic, George? That's just the reason I've always been so jealous of you—because everybody always likes you."

"I don't suppose you'd be interested in trading personalities?" George asked.

"Call Mother and Father, George. Richard and I will wait right here."

George took a deep breath. "You're not going to let me get out of this, are you?"

"No."

"What if I say the wrong thing?"

"You won't. Just tell them the truth, and the rest will fall into place."

George walked stiffly over to the phone. After speaking with the operator for a moment, he paused. He glanced over at Christy and sent her a forced, tense smile.

A moment later, Christy heard him say just the right thing:

"Hello, Mother? It's me, George. I . . . I'm sorry I made you worry. And I love you."

❧ Sixteen ❧

It's so beautiful," Christy whispered, thinking of the more modest Flora College, in Red Springs, North Carolina, where she'd gotten her training to be a teacher.

George smiled wryly at his sister. "That's because you're on the outside, looking in. When you're sitting in a classroom, agonizing over one of Mr. Burns's Latin exams, it doesn't seem quite so charming."

They were standing outside the tall bronze gate at the entrance to the Bristol Academy. The school itself was a huge white mansion surrounded by manicured grounds. Four separate dormitory buildings flanked it on either side.

"How do we get inside?" Christy asked.

"The guard will let us in," Richard replied. "At least, I *think* he will. Could be George and I are considered criminals by now."

"I still say we should have made an appointment," George argued. It was a lame attempt to stall, but he figured it was worth a try.

"I'm sure the headmaster will be anxious to hear what you have to say," Christy said.

George gazed up at the imposing main building. "I don't know, Sis. I have a bad feeling about this."

"What did Mother and Father tell you to do when you spoke to them?" Christy asked.

"Well, mostly Mother just cried," George said, still stinging at the memory. "And Father didn't have much to say. You know how he is—he just said he was confident I'd do the right thing. But I'm just not sure this *is* the right thing. If we keep our mouths shut, at least we can be sure that Richard will stay in school. This way, I'm afraid we'll both get expelled, and what good will that do?"

Richard held up the small fabric satchel he was carrying. "You're forgetting one thing— the money I stole. One way or another, George, I'm giving it back."

"You could just leave it by the headmaster's door in the middle of the night," George suggested. "No one would ever know how it got there."

"George," Christy said firmly, hands on her hips, "you're stalling."

"That's right. I am." George grinned

sheepishly. "And I was very much hoping you wouldn't notice."

"I'm sure this is the right thing to do," Christy said. "But in the end, it must be your decision."

George looked from his sister to Richard and back again. "Well, I can see I'm outnumbered." He turned to Richard. "Come on, pal. Let's get this over with, before I lose my nerve."

— — —

"Well, well, well. This is a surprise."

Even sitting behind his desk, Mr. Koller was an imposing man. Beefy and balding, he had a thick mustache and a deep baritone voice that seemed to shake the walls.

His office, too, was intimidating. Three walls were lined to the ceiling with leather-bound books, and Mr. Koller's mahogany desk seemed as large as a new Ford automobile. The family photograph on his desk was the only sign of a gentler man.

George had only been here once before, when he'd enrolled at the academy. His parents had been with him then. Their proud faces were etched in his memory.

It burned to think of the pain he'd heard in their voices today—the hurt and betrayal. How could he have let them down so badly? He'd meant well, of course. But it was frightening to think that you could try to do the right thing, and still end up in such an awful mess.

"And to what do I owe the honor of this visit?" Mr. Koller inquired, arms crossed over his chest.

"I . . . we . . . well, George and I have something to say," Richard began in a thin, halting voice.

"I'm all ears."

Richard and George exchanged looks. Richard was trembling. His face was ashen.

"Might this have something to do with the mystery of the vanishing money?" Mr. Koller leaned forward, elbows on his desk. He fixed his stare on George. "And the mystery of Master Huddleston's sudden and inexplicable disappearance shortly thereafter?"

"Yes," George said. "It's about the money. You see, there's been . . . well, a bit of a misunderstanding about all that."

"A misunderstanding. Is that what it's called now? You break in to my office, steal from this academy, and then call it a misunderstanding?" Mr. Koller bellowed.

George swallowed hard as Mr. Koller stared sternly at the two of them. "My word . . . What's next? What are—"

"I took it!" Richard blurted, placing the sack of money on the headmaster's desk. "I took it! George didn't. If you're going to expel anybody, it ought to be me!"

The words came out in a terrible rush. When Richard was done, he almost looked relieved.

"It's a little more complicated than that," George began, but Mr. Koller interrupted.

"Yes, it always is," he said sarcastically. He pursed his lips, gazing at Richard skeptically, as if he didn't quite believe he was capable of the crime. "And how exactly did you get into my office, if you don't mind my asking? Just so I can prevent any further incursions."

"I picked the lock," Richard admitted. "I used a piece of wire. Took a while, but I got it eventually."

"Yes, indeed, you did."

Mr. Koller leaned back in his chair, regarding each boy thoughtfully. It was impossible to tell what he was thinking. A slight smile seemed to lurk behind that mustache, but it could just as easily have been a sneer. Still, he didn't seem all *that* angry. No books had been thrown, no threats had been made. Perhaps he was going to go lightly on the boys, chalk it up to a silly prank and nothing more.

"The thing is," George spoke up, "Richard had a very good reason for taking the money, Mr. Koller. You see—"

"A good reason?" Mr. Koller repeated in a stern voice. "Are you suggesting there is ever a good reason for thievery? Do the words

'Thou shalt not steal' ring a bell for you, Master Huddleston?"

"I . . . well, of course they do. I know it's wrong to steal. And so does Richard. But sometimes there are circumstances—"

"There are *no* circumstances that justify stealing!" Mr. Koller bellowed. "And while we're on the subject, there are no circumstances that justify lying, either. Am I safe in assuming that you had knowledge of Mr. Benton's actions?"

"Yes, I did."

"But only after I'd confessed to George about what I'd done," Richard clarified. "He had nothing to do with this, Mr. Koller. You have to believe me!"

"You're asking me to believe a young man who broke into my office and stole money belonging to the academy?"

"George was only trying to protect me," Richard said weakly. "He was just trying to be a good friend."

"A good friend would have promptly turned you in to the authorities."

"George *did* try to talk me into returning the money. He did. But I was so sure I was right. . . ."

For a long time, Mr. Koller said nothing. He fiddled with his inkwell. He stared at the ceiling. He toyed with his mustache.

Quietly, he ordered, "Count the money."

George and Richard looked at each other. Gingerly, George reached for the small sack. He felt as if he was putting his hand in hot coals as he slowly pulled out the money. He did not look at Mr. Koller, but directly at the money as he counted every cent into Richard's trembling hands, occasionally pausing for Richard to stack the money on the headmaster's desk. When he was through he glanced up at Mr. Koller, who seemed to be deep in thought.

The tension was unbearable. But if he was taking so long to make a decision, George reasoned, that had to be a good sign, didn't it? Perhaps he was trying to decide what punishment would be appropriate. *I'll do anything,* George thought, *if he'll just give me another chance.*

At last Mr. Koller stood. He looked at each boy with a mixture of regret and resignation.

"I'm sorry, gentlemen, but you simply leave me no choice. The Bristol Academy is known for upholding not only the highest academic standards, but the highest moral standards. And I'm afraid you two do not meet our requirements. Effective immediately, you are both expelled."

❧ Seventeen ❧

Y ou're pacing again."

Christy smiled at the headmaster's secretary, Miss Murkoff. "I'm sorry. I can't seem to stop myself."

It seemed as if she'd been waiting here for hours, but in truth, it had only been a short while. Behind the closed door that led to Mr. Koller's office, Christy heard a deep, rumbling male voice.

Once again she tried to imagine how things were going on the other side of that door. Were Richard and George going to be able to stay here at the academy? Christy had been so sure that urging George to tell the truth would solve matters. But now, as the minutes ticked by, she was almost beginning to have some doubts.

"Would you like some more tea?" asked Miss Murkoff, a slender woman whose white hair was pulled back in a tidy bun.

"Oh, no, I'm fine. You've been so kind already, keeping me company." While Christy waited, Miss Murkoff had entertained her with stories about the academy, the staff, and the many students she'd seen come and go over the years.

Miss Murkoff glanced at the headmaster's door. "I do hope everything works out for George. He's such a fine boy. I've always had a soft spot in my heart for him. On my birthday, he brought me a bouquet of paper flowers."

"He does love to do his magic tricks," Christy said.

Mr. Koller's voice rose, muffled behind the heavy door. Christy bit her lip anxiously.

"Don't worry," Miss Murkoff said. "Mr. Koller's bark is worse than his bite." She paused. "Usually, anyway. He can be stern when he has to be."

"I remember George telling me once that all the boys are afraid of him."

"Well, I suppose that's true. He doesn't tolerate misbehavior, and he expects our students to follow the rules. But he has to be that way, in order to keep things from getting out of control. You can imagine how rowdy boys this age can be."

Christy managed a smile, recalling some of George's antics over the years. "Yes, I suppose it's hard to keep order."

"Still, he's a fine man, Mr. Koller. I'm sure he'll be fair with your brother."

"I guess that's all I can ask for."

"I've worked here for many, many years," Miss Murkoff said. "And I've come to respect Mr. Koller tremendously."

Again Mr. Koller's voice rose. It was hard for Christy to catch any words, but the tone was unmistakably angry.

Miss Murkoff gave a small, wry smile, "Yes, I respect him tremendously. Even if he *can* be a bit gruff sometimes."

Just then, the door slowly opened. George and Richard emerged.

"Well?" Christy asked, but she could tell from their expressions what the answer was.

She threw her arms around George. "I'm so sorry," she whispered.

George shrugged. "Mr. Koller's right. We deserve to be punished for what happened. I only wish Richard could have stayed. . . ."

"It's my fault this whole thing happened," Richard said. "I don't deserve to stay."

As they departed, Miss Murkoff gave a small wave. "Goodbye, boys. I'll miss you." She clucked her tongue softly. "I really did love those magic flowers."

They walked slowly to the dormitory and collected their belongings. As they headed down the long walk to the front gate of the academy, no one spoke.

At last Richard said, "You were right about one thing, Miss Huddleston. I do feel better. I told the truth and returned the money, and that was the right thing to do. But now, I've ruined George's life. And my sister's right back where she started . . ."

The guard opened the gate and they exited.

"My life isn't ruined, pal," George said, slapping Richard on the back. "Why, who knows what adventures await me, now that I'm free from the confines of the Bristol Academy? It always *was* a stodgy old school. From here on out, I intend to learn my lessons in the school of life."

But despite his optimistic manner, George couldn't disguise his fear. Christy patted her brother on the shoulder. "I really thought it would turn out differently. Did you explain the whole story to Mr. Koller?"

"As much as we could," George said, "but Mr. Koller did most of the talking."

Behind them, an automobile approached. Its horn gave a loud honk. Christy spun around to see a familiar sight. "It's Father," she cried, "and Mother, too!"

The car came to a stop behind them and Mr. and Mrs. Huddleston leapt out. They each took turns warmly embracing Christy and

George. Mrs. Huddleston even gave Richard an extra-long hug.

"You shouldn't have come," George said uncomfortably.

"We wanted to, son," Mr. Huddleston replied.

Mrs. Huddleston cleared her throat, and Mr. Huddleston added, "Well, if the truth be told, we were angry at first—and disappointed. But the more we thought about the way your sister was supporting you . . . we knew we had to follow her example."

"Have you spoken to Mr. Koller yet?" Mrs. Huddleston asked.

"We were expelled," George muttered, head hung low.

"Oh my," Mrs. Huddleston said.

"Please don't blame George for any of this," Richard interjected. "It's really all my fault."

"We know the whole story, Richard," Mr. Huddleston assured him. "I'm just sorry it had to end this way."

"Maybe . . . " Christy paused, glancing back at the sprawling academy buildings, "maybe it doesn't have to end this way."

"What do you mean, Sis?" George asked.

"I'm going back to the headmaster's," Christy said firmly.

"Christy, dear," said Mrs. Huddleston, "if your brother couldn't convince Mr. Koller to give him a second chance, then I hardly think you'll have better luck."

"George may be charming, Mother," Christy said, winking at her brother, "but I've learned a thing or two about people in the past year. Wait for me here. I won't be long."

❧ Eighteen ❧

W hy, Miss Huddleston," Miss Murkoff exclaimed when Christy returned, "did you forget something?"

"Actually, I did," Christy said breathlessly. "I forgot to request a brief meeting with Mr. Koller."

"It's getting late, and he's got another appointment in five minutes." Miss Murkoff consulted her calendar and clucked her tongue. "Peter Smithers—a real discipline problem."

"I promise it will only take a minute or two."

"Let me see if Mr. Koller will meet with you. Generally, after expelling a student . . . well, you understand. He prefers not to meet with the family." Miss Murkoff smiled at Christy. "But I'll tell him what a nice chat you and I had, and maybe I can convince him to see you."

Miss Murkoff knocked on the headmaster's door and slipped inside. A few moments later, she emerged. "He'll see you," she said, "but just for a minute."

As Christy stepped into Mr. Koller's office, she could imagine the fear her brother and Richard must have felt. Mr. Koller was an impressive figure—even more so when he greeted her in his booming voice.

"To begin with, Miss Huddleston, I'm afraid I must tell you, that in my many years as headmaster, I have never changed my mind about an expulsion," he began, gesturing her toward a leather chair. "I don't make such decisions lightly, I can assure you. And the gravity of the offense committed by your brother and his roommate cannot be overlooked."

"I understand," Christy said. Her voice sounded tinny and small after Mr. Koller's words. "And I was as upset and disappointed by what they did as anyone. I firmly believe they should be punished, too."

"Then you came here to tell me we're in agreement?" Mr. Koller pulled at his mustache. "I must say that's unusual behavior for a family member."

"Well, we're in agreement, but not entirely," Christy said. "Mr. Koller, did Richard or George tell you *why* the money was stolen?"

Mr. Koller shook his head. "No."

"Richard's family has been having money problems," Christy said. "His sister broke her leg a few months ago, and there was no money to have it properly cared for. The leg set badly, and the girl is in constant pain. Now the only hope is for her to have expensive surgery."

Mr. Koller swiveled his chair and looked out the window behind his desk. "I'm sorry to hear that."

"That's the reason Richard took the money, Mr. Koller," Christy continued. "I know it doesn't in any way excuse his behavior, and Richard knows it, too. That's why he came back here. To return the money and set things right—even though he believed that money may well have been his sister's only hope."

Mr. Koller turned back to Christy. "As sympathetic as I am to Richard's plight, I cannot excuse such behavior. He's lucky I didn't turn him in to the authorities."

"I'm not asking you to excuse his behavior." Christy went to the edge of Mr. Koller's desk, her voice pleading. "All I'm saying is the punishment should fit the crime. This is Richard's one chance at obtaining an education—and quite possibly, George's. Haven't other boys at Bristol been punished in other ways?"

"Most certainly. With detentions or with work assignments on the grounds. But those aren't boys who stole money from under my very nose and then lied about it. I'm sorry, Miss Huddleston, but any leniency is strictly out of the question."

"Mr. Koller," Christy said so quietly that the headmaster had to lean forward to hear her, "sometimes students do things that embarrass their teachers. I know it must be distressing to have a student do this, as you said, 'right under your nose.'"

"Yes," he admitted. "And, I know where you are headed with this conversation, but I would not let embarrassment influence my decision," he said indignantly.

"I guess there's nothing I can say to change your mind?"

"If I listened to every pleading family member who came through this door, discipline at Bristol would be impossible. Now, if you'll excuse me, I have business to attend to." Mr. Koller gave a slight smile. "I must say, however, that I admire your sisterly loyalty."

Christy's gaze fell on a family photograph on the corner of Mr. Koller's desk. "Is that your sister, by any chance?"

"Why . . . why, yes." Mr. Koller gazed fondly at the sepia-toned photo. "But how did you guess—?"

"Miss Murkoff told me a lot about you while I was waiting."

"Yes, she can be quite the talker."

"She mentioned that your sister was paralyzed in an accident when she was four."

Mr. Koller nodded. "It was a hard time," he said softly.

"What if, as a young man, you'd thought there was a way you could have helped her walk again?" Christy asked.

Mr. Koller stared at the photograph as if he were traveling through time. "I suppose," he said, "if I'd thought I could do something to help her, I would have done it, no matter what."

The admission seemed to surprise him. He sat very still, eyes closed. The only sound in the room was the ticking of his grandfather clock.

At last he opened his eyes and turned to Christy. A smile slowly formed on his face. "My, my, but you are a persuasive young woman. May I ask what you do for a living?"

"I'm the teacher at a mission school in Tennessee."

Mr. Koller took a deep breath and stood. "I'm going to give your brother and his friend a second chance, Miss Huddleston. They will do so much work around here and suffer through so many detentions that they may wish I hadn't let them come back. But if they persevere and don't stray again, I may just see you again someday . . . at their graduation ceremony. Thanks, in large measure, to one very loyal and loving sister."

Christy smiled at the headmaster. "You are a fair man, Mr. Koller," she said.

"I try," he replied. Then after a pause, he gently said, "Would you tell me more about Richard's family?"

❧ Nineteen ❧

Well?" George asked.

"How'd it go?" Richard questioned softly.

The two boys and Christy's parents were leaning against the parked automobile, waiting expectantly.

Christy cleared her throat, her face grave. "I'm sure you realize what a stern man Mr. Koller is," she began.

"He's tough," Richard agreed.

"The toughest," said George.

"And I'm sure you both realize the gravity of your crimes."

Both boys nodded.

"So you didn't have any luck?" George asked in a resigned voice.

"Well, I didn't say that." Christy broke into a grin. "Let's just say you're going to be facing lots of punishment. But you're staying in school. Both of you."

"Christy!" George lifted her into his arms and whirled her around till she was dizzy. "You're amazing! You are the most amazing, incredible, wonderful sister—"

"George, please put me down before I get sick," Christy instructed.

Richard gave her an awkward hug. "I don't know how to thank you," he said.

"I'll tell you how you can both thank me," Christy said as she straightened her dress. "Do not get into any more trouble between now and graduation. Understand?"

George saluted her. "You have my word."

"And mine," Richard added softly.

"Richard," Mrs. Huddleston said. "You don't seem all that happy, dear."

"Oh, I am. I'm really grateful to Christy for getting me a second chance. It's just that I was thinking about Abigail, my little sister. I feel sort of guilty about the idea of continuing school. Maybe if I got a job instead . . ."

"Give it some time, Richard," Christy advised. "Doctor MacNeill said he was going to get in touch with some of his friends. Maybe something will work out."

"And we could talk to some people from our church about putting together a fund for Abigail," Mr. Huddleston offered.

"Don't give up yet, Richard," George advised. "By now, it should be pretty obvious that my sister is capable of magical feats."

"Turns out you're not the only magician in the family," Christy said with a wink.

～～～

Five weeks later, Mr. Pentland brought Christy a letter one afternoon just as school was about to let out for the day. She read the return address and gasped.

"It's from George!" she exclaimed. "I can't believe it. He hardly *ever* writes letters!"

While the children gathered around, she tore open the envelope excitedly. This was one letter she definitely couldn't wait to read.

Christy was surprised to find two letters in the envelope—one from George and one from Richard. Slowly, she began to read George's out loud:

> **Dear Christy,**
> Surprise! Bet you never thought you'd see a letter from yours truly. But I wanted to write and say thank you, once again, for everything you did for Richard and me.
> Mr. Koller's assigned us to every work detail you can imagine—caring for the grounds, washing blackboards, even helping in the dining room. (Tell Doc MacNeill my cooking skills have definitely improved.)

But we're grateful for the punishment. We know it means a second chance at school, and we're not going to make any mistakes this time.

We've got a few days off next month, and Mr. Koller's even letting Richard and me leave the school grounds. Richard's going home to visit his family. But, I'll let him tell you his news in his own letter.

I thought I might head back to Cutter Gap for another visit—that is, if you'll have me. I promise not to disrupt class or otherwise misbehave.

Your loving brother,
George

P.S. I really will try to write more often.

"George is a-comin!" Creed cried. "George is a-comin' back!"

The children laughed and applauded, and Christy was proud to realize she didn't feel the least bit jealous. In fact, she felt like laughing and applauding herself.

Only Ruby Mae seemed a bit skeptical. "I'll believe it when I see it," she said, arms crossed over her chest. "That George is a most unreliable boy, if'n you ask me."

"Read the other letter, Miz Christy," someone urged.

Christy turned to Richard's letter and read:

Dear Miss Huddleston,

I am writing on behalf of my family to thank you, Doctor MacNeill, the people at the mission, and your parents' congregation for your help.

Thanks to your generosity, and the generosity of Doctor MacNeill's fellow physicians, Abigail is now recovering from her surgery of last week. She is in some pain, but the doctors tell us they expect a complete recovery. And Abigail is confident she'll be up and around by her birthday next month.

And thanks to a contact of your father's, my father has begun a new job at the railroad office in town. It has been a long time since I have seen him so happy, or so full of hope. And it's all thanks to this miracle you helped bring about.

It has been a long time since I have felt so hopeful, too.

Thank you again for all you have done.

Yours truly,
Richard Benton

Christy tucked the letter back into its envelope. "Don't thank me, Richard," she whispered. "Thank God. He's the miracle worker."

❧ Twenty ❧

I just cannot wait to see that charming young man again," Miss Ida said excitedly as she bustled about the mission kitchen a few weeks later. "I do hope he gets here soon. I have such a feast planned."

"So you've forgiven George for everything?" Christy asked.

Miss Ida grinned. "Well, I was a little miffed about the way he lied to us. But now that the whole story's out, and he's being properly punished at school . . . well, it seems like it's time to forgive and forget."

"He is a little late," Christy said, glancing out the window. "It's nearly dark, and he should have made it here by now. Maybe I should have gone to meet him at the train station."

"He'll be here," said Doctor MacNeill. "Don't you worry. He wouldn't dare miss Miss Ida's cooking."

"Speaking of missing persons," said Miss Alice as she finished setting the table, "has anyone seen Ruby Mae?"

"Not for an hour or two," Christy replied. "Maybe she's feeding Prince."

"Or maybe," a voice called from the parlor, "she's assisting George the Magnificent in his amazing magical extravaganza!"

"That sounded like . . ." Christy began.

She ran into the parlor. There stood George, dressed in his best suit and wearing a tall, black top hat. Next to him stood Ruby Mae, wearing a sparkling bead turban and pink feather cape.

"Ladies and gentlemen," said George in his smoothest magician voice, "allow me to introduce my incredible assistant, Ruby Mae the Remarkable!"

Ruby Mae took a low bow.

"But how long have you been here?" Christy cried, rushing over to give her brother a big hug.

"Long enough to prepare a wonderful magic show for your entertainment," George replied with a wink. "We've been practicing over at the schoolhouse. My assistant and I are prepared to delight and amaze you."

"How about if you delight and amaze us *after* dinner?" Miss Alice suggested. "Miss Ida's put together a wonderful meal in your honor, George."

"How about it, Ruby Mae?" George asked.

"Sounds good to me. My stomach's a-rumblin' somethin' fierce," Ruby Mae replied. "Magic is hard work." She headed for the dining room. "Well, come on, everybody. Let's dig in!"

As everyone gathered around the table, Ruby Mae tugged on Christy's arm. "Told ya he'd be back," she said. She cast George a flirtatious smile. "You're so lucky to have a brother like him. I just wish he could stay forever. Don't you, Miz Christy?"

Christy glanced across the table. George was in the middle of telling a joke. As usual, all eyes were on her brother.

He would always be charming. He would always be the center of attention. And he would always be a little unpredictable.

And she would always love him.

"You know, Ruby Mae," Christy said, "I wish he could stay forever, too."

About the Author

Catherine Marshall

With *Christy*, Catherine Marshall LeSourd (1914–1983) created one of the world's most widely read and best-loved classics. Published in 1967, the book spent 39 weeks on the New York Times bestseller list. With an estimated 30 million Americans having read it, *Christy* is now approaching its 90th printing and has sold more than eight million copies. Although a novel, *Christy* is in fact a thinly-veiled biography of Catherine's mother, Leonora Wood.

Catherine Marshall LeSourd also authored *A Man Called Peter*, which has sold more than four million copies. It is an American bestseller, portraying the love between a dynamic man and his God, and the tender, romantic love between a man and the girl he married.

Another one of Catherine's books is *Julie,* a powerful, sweeping novel of love and adventure, courage and commitment, tragedy and triumph, in a Pennsylvania town during the Great Depression. Catherine also authored many other devotional books of encouragement.

THE CHRISTY® JUVENILE FICTION SERIES
You'll want to read them all!

Based upon Catherine Marshall's international bestseller
Christy®, this new series contains expanded adventures
filled with romance, intrigue, and excitement.

VOLUME ONE
(ISBN 1-4003-0772-4)

#1—The Bridge to Cutter Gap
Nineteen-year-old Christy leaves her family to teach
at a mission school in the Great Smoky Mountains.
On the other side of an icy bridge lie excitement,
adventure, and maybe even the man of her dreams
. . . but can she survive a life-and-death struggle
when she falls into the rushing waters below?

#2—Silent Superstitions
Christy's students are suddenly afraid to come to
school. Is what Granny O'Teale says true? Is their
teacher cursed? Will the children's fears and the
adults' superstitions force Christy to abandon her
dreams and return to North Carolina?

#3—The Angry Intruder
Someone wants Christy to leave Cutter Gap, and
they'll stop at nothing. Mysterious pranks soon turn
dangerous. Could a student be the culprit? When
Christy confronts the late-night intruder, will it be a
face she knows?

#8—Family Secrets
Bob Allen and many of the residents of Cutter Gap
are upset when a black family, the Washingtons,
moves in near the Allens' property. When a series of
threatening incidents befall the Washingtons, Christy
steps in to help. But it's a clue in the Washingtons'
family Bible that may hold the real key to peace and
acceptance.

#9—Mountain Madness
When Christy travels alone to a nearby mountain,
she vows to discover the truth behind the terrifying
legend of a strange mountain creature. But what she
finds, at first seems worse than she ever imagined!

VOLUME FOUR
(ISBN 1-4003-0775-9)

#10—Stage Fright
As Christy's students are preparing for a school play,
she reveals her dream to act on stage herself. Little
does she know that Doctor MacNeill's aunt is the
artistic director of the Knoxville theater. Before long,
just as Christy is about to debut on stage, several
mysterious incidents threaten both her dreams and
her pride!

#11—Goodbye, Sweet Prince
Prince, the mission's stallion, is sold to a cruel
owner, then disappears. Christy Huddleston and her
students are heartsick. Is there any way to reclaim
the magnificent horse?

#12—Brotherly Love
Everyone is delighted when Christy's younger brother,
George Huddleston, visits Christy at the Cutter Gap

Mission. But the delight ends when George reveals that he has been expelled from school for stealing. Can Christy summon the love and faith to help her brother do the right thing?